SHORT STORIES
and TALL TALES

An Irish Story Book

J AMES W OODS

BALBOA.
PRESS

A DIVISION OF HAY HOUSE

Balboa Press books may be ordered through booksellers or by contacting:

Balboa Press
A Division of Hay House
1663 Liberty Drive
Bloomington, IN 47403
www.balboapress.com
1 (877) 407-4847

Because of the dynamic nature of the Internet, any web addresses or links contained in this book may have changed since publication and may no longer be valid. The views expressed in this work are solely those of the author and do not necessarily reflect the views of the publisher, and the publisher hereby disclaims any responsibility for them.

The author of this book does not dispense medical advice or prescribe the use of any technique as a form of treatment for physical, emotional, or medical problems without the advice of a physician, either directly or indirectly. The intent of the author is only to offer information of a general nature to help you in your quest for emotional and spiritual well-being. In the event you use any of the information in this book for yourself, which is your constitutional right, the author and the publisher assume no responsibility for your actions.

Any people depicted in stock imagery provided by Thinkstock are models, and such images are being used for illustrative purposes only. Certain stock imagery © Thinkstock.

Print information available on the last page.

ISBN: 978-1-5043-5460-8 (sc)
ISBN: 978-1-5043-5461-5 (e)

Balboa Press rev. date: 05/26/2016

DEDICATION

"Tall Tales and Short Stories" is my second book, following on from "Across the Sheugh" that was published at the beginning of 2015. This new book is different from the first in that the tall tales and short stories included herein are totally fiction – based on stories I have been told and not on adventures experienced.

These stories and tales were compiled at the same time that I was writing my first book. Because of this fact it has been easier to finalise and sort these stories into a book format. For this I want to thank all those members of my family who have had the patience and perseverence to listen to these stories and approve them for inclusion.

Jim Woods

CONTENTS

INTRODUCTION

Ireland past and present is known to the world as the "Isle of Saints and Scholars". There is also good reason for it to be known as "The Land of Mists and Myths." Wherever you go in the island of Ireland you will meet some person who can tell you a local story of mystery, adventure, ghosts, fairies, murder or humorous encounters. It is no lie to say that the Irish were blessed with "The gift of the Gab" for the vast majority of us have braved the danger and kissed the "Blarney Stone".

The stories contained in this collection are new and all are set in the island of Ireland. They will include Fairies, Leprechauns, Banshees, Pookas, Pig-Dogs and wide variety of magical beings. There will be stories of Witches, Warlocks, and Wise-men. To some they may just be Tall Tales, but they are all Short Stories and there are some who will maintain there is an element of truth in them all.

As I began to compile this collection of Irish-based stories into a completed book, I was drawn back to that time when the idea of writing stories first entered into my mind. Although I had always been a fervent reader of books, since I had first learned to read from "Dick and Dora Books" in Primary School, there had never been a time when I considered myself capable of writing any story. In my mid-fifties I had returned to favored territory and once again began reading a collection of stories penned by the late Irish author, John B. Keane. One of the stories written by this noted author included a short piece on the theme of 'Bucket Handles'. The fact that Keane was able to write so interestingly and humorously about such mundane pieces of equipment actually inspired me to try short story writing for myself.

Keane's writing is very descriptive, but interesting, in the way he used simple language and simple structures of composition. Perhaps one of his greatest gifts, however, was the ease in which he included his native Kerry humor to enhance the tale. It is not an easy talent to replicate and I wouldn't even attempt the feat. But, all my adult life I told stories to my younger cousins, then my own children and, now, my grandchildren. Some stories were enhancements of stories I had heard, while others were stories that were born out of my own imagination. As I read the stories of Keane, O'Flaherty, and others I began to think that I too could record my tales. Moreover, I was encouraged to be more observant of the world around me and record those observations for the future. If John B. Keane could write about 'Bucket Handles' maybe I could write something about 'Buckets'.

First things first, I called upon 'Google Images' to give me an idea of the range of buckets that are available to us. It was an amazing revelation. But, unexpectedly, my mind began to reflect on just how much buckets could be compared to story writing. Just like the humble bucket a story is created from a variety of materials, each of which is suited to a particular task. The bucket can be constructed from materials such as metal and plastic, wood, and even leather. A story is constructed from experience, observation, imagination, and even emotion. All of these things create the environment and the action that we place in our story. Our bucket becomes our story because we put into it those things that give us life and those things we may not want observed. However, like the humble bucket, we often take our stories for granted, filling them only half-way with material.

Have you ever considered what would you do if you found that you had not got a bucket to assist you with the task you are about to undertake? Like myself, you would probably seek out something that would perform exactly the same task; namely carrying water, cement, sand, ashes, coal, kindling, and a host of other materials. There are, however, very few other items into which we would place our food scraps, or the waste produced by our pets. This fact alone gives us ample demonstration of the reasoning behind our need to purchase more than one bucket. After all what would we us to carry meal, carrots, spring onions, potatoes, and other foodstuffs harvested from our gardens? None of us, surely, would put them into the same bucket in which we harvested our pets' faeces and food waste? So it is with the creation of a story or stories that will illuminate the emotions and intentions of the author. The variety of stories based upon the one theme can be numerous, pointing out clearly to us all that, as it is with buckets, there are "different courses for different horses." The author will write a variety of stories, written from a variety of viewpoints, that will answer the needs of both author and audience alike.

To begin with, I considered all those old stories which had been related to me by various family members. As I ran my mind through all of those stories I became amazed by the amount of myth, and magic that they contained. They were more than just simple fantasy tales. They were a rainbow collection of quite believable stories about ordinary people. What was not so ordinary, however, was their encounters with various spirits, both good and evil. These spirits were, each one of them, known to an Irish child of my generation and their existence was widely believed throughout Ireland.

We can again compare such stories to the variety of buckets that are put before us, and from which we must make our choices. The buckets are every color of the rainbow - green, red, blue, orange, brown, purple, grey, black, yellow, and metallic. We choose the color to suit the environment in which we want to use it, and then fill it with items that will make us feel better. You have, undoubtedly, seen buckets filled with beautiful flowers or shrubs that make our gardens much more attractive. It is also likely that you have used a bucket to remove waste and dirt to make your environment brighter and more clear. In many Irish households, even in these modern times, the story still holds a valued place. These stories come in their own colors and tones, such as cold, dark, warm, comforting, bright and refreshing. They can bring calm to the anxious, hope to those who have no light in their life, and comfort to those who have felt only sorrow.

As we stand and admire the many forms in which the bucket has been created we must admire those men and women who struggled to bring their ideas to reality. In the same manner we must appreciate those persons who have created and built their stories, as well as those in our society who maintain the time-honored tradition of story-telling. These narrators are like the handles of the buckets and without them the buckets are next to useless. There may be rope handles, grip handles, ornate handles, or just simple metal handles. In the same way stories have various types of narrators, or handles. There are those who prefer to emphasize the message, to dramatize the tale they tell, or simply relate it as it has been written. It is they who point out the life-lessons to be learned, the warnings to be heeded, and the myriad of valuable insights that these stories contain.

Have you, like I have, stood before an array of books on shelves and struggled with the task of deciding which of these might provide the best story to read? What criteria do you use in your decision making? Is it size, author, cover, or price? Just as it is when choosing a bucket the final choice will come down to value for money and if it does the job we need it to do. The story tellers who find themselves before a wide-range of stories need to ponder carefully before deciding which of them will fulfill the needs of the audience to whom it will be related. Things which he, or she, might consider are the age structure of the audience, the educational level, and the possibility of positive interaction.

Before we move on to this particular collection of stories there is one more area which we might just explore. In recent years, for example, the word 'bucket' has gained a wider descriptive use in our language. Cars now have "Bucket-seats", while the fashion industry has created a 'fad' for "Bucket-hats." The travel and leisure industry has increasingly put forward the term "Bucket List" to describe all those things a person wishes to experience in their life-time. Much in the same way stories and their genres have been given descriptions deemed to be more appropriate to the modern reading public. Today we do not just have fantasy novels and romance novels. These are further divided into erotic fantasy, action fantasy, historical romances, gay romance, and many other groupings. There are "Young-Adult" stories, "Steam Punk" books, and "Graphic Novels", etc. Many of these terms were not used ten or fifteen years ago, but it is exciting to use such widespread collections of stories that writers want to record and pass on.

All of these things are further proof that the humble story can help facilitate discussion on many subjects of life that people usually prefer to keep at a distance. Many modern story-tellers have helped bring to the fore a wide-range of social problems and opened discussion on difficult topics. With censorship virtually abandoned we hear more about the problems of Old Age, Death, Terminal Illness, Abortion, Sex and Sexuality, Depression, Suicide, and Paedophilia. Most readers will be relieved to hear that the vast majority of these discussion points do not find their way into the stories of this collection. But, there is one request I think I should ask of the reader and that is to act just as you would when you go to choose a bucket, namely look and examine the entire range placed before you before selecting the story, or stories, that you like most.

THE THORN

Malachy McCann was ninety-two years old and proud of being the oldest living native still resident in the village of Ardshee. There was not one person in the village who could be certain of just how old Malachy was. Indeed, there were very few of the village's residents who even remembered him as a young man since he had managed to outlive many of his contemporaries. Nevertheless, despite his great age Malachy still took a great care of his appearance, especially his thick, silvery grey hair, which he ensured was trimmed to perfection every month. He may have been a little bit unsteady on those aging legs, but he stubbornly refused to use any type of walking aid. Moreover, for a man of his great age his mind remained clear and fully alert. There was nothing he enjoyed more than a good debate with the other men of the Parish on the question of Gaelic football, and the other things that he believed were important to life. Among these other things, Malachy held the local traditions and superstitions of the countryside to his heart. Indeed, there were many occasions when Malachy insisted that his longevity was due, in large part, to the presence of a lone, hawthorn bush that grew on a small piece of land that he owned.

Some readers may already be aware of the fact that the hawthorn tree has, from earliest times, been treated with the greatest of respect by those Irish people who hold on to their ancient traditions. In the various areas of this island this simple, but wondrous, tree has been given a variety of names by the people. In some places it is known as "The Lone Bush", in other places "The Gentle Bush", or even as "The Thorn." It is very rare, however, to hear it being referred to by its legendary title, "The Fairy Tree."

There are some Irish people who would consider the very fact that I am putting these things in writing as being an act of disrespect to the "Little People", who live in and around the branches and roots of the hawthorn. Any person foolish enough to cut down the hawthorn or remove any of its branches will undoubtedly bring down a terrible fate upon themselves. Even slight damage might bring a person bad luck, while destruction may bring a death curse upon the person who causes the injury to be done. There are those who have extensive knowledge of these things and will warn the unwary that they should not even hang items from the branches of the hawthorn. They say that such items disturb the peace of "the little people" who congregate and live around the tree. It is advised that no person should ever want to disturb these spirits, or even cause their anger to be aroused. They are mischievous beings who will plague those who would dare arouse them until madness and even death follows.

Malachy McCann was a man of the country, steeped in the living traditions and superstitions of Ireland. His farm was only a small holding and the survival of this property, Malachy believed, was the result of his respect for the "Fairy People." Small acreage, however, did not preclude Malachy from considering himself to be a property-owner. Like most of the property in Ardshee and surrounding district Malachy's land had been passed down through the generations to him. Tradition called for the farm to be passed on to the youngest son, and this was the route that Malachy had wanted to follow. This, however, was no longer possible as his youngest son had tragically passed away many years before.

Malachy continued to work upon the small area of land he owned, although age had weakened him and limited the work he was now able to do. He cared for four large, healthy beef cattle, which grazed upon the grass in the field. At the same time he reared a dozen plump chickens and two ducks that roamed freely in the grounds around Malachy's small thatched cottage. In comparison to some farms in the area Malachy's small-holding was very limited in size, but it took all of his energy and experience to maintain it to the high standard he had achieved. Malachy McCann, however, was one man who had never avoided hard work in his life and worked to the very limits of his age. In one area of his land to the side of his cottage he planted "Kerr's Pinks" potatoes, which he particularly liked to eat. In the Ardshee area, in fact, Malachy was considered by some to be a bit of a connoisseur of the humble potato, and his advice was often sought by other growers in the Parish. But, the major credit to his stamina was undoubtedly the regularity with which he could be seen cleaning ditches on his land, or digging post holes for his fences.

Come rain, hail or sunshine you could set your watch by the time Malachy would leave his cottage and head into the centre of the village. There were those who jokingly called this activity, "Old Malachy's Daily Pilgrimage", because his walk took him to his favorite bar stool at "Healey's" Public Bar. It was, in fact, such a common event that Charlie Healey would begin, as the bar clock struck twelve, to put together Malachy's regular drink order in readiness for his appearance. At four minutes past twelve the old man would come through the main door of the bar and sit upon his stool. There he would pour out some of the "Harp" Lager from the bottle into a glass and then add a small amount of water into his glass of "Powers'" Whisky.

The bottle of lager was always taken from the shelf and never from the cooler. Malachy did not like the modern affectation for ice cold beer precisely because it was a modern idea and had never been done when he first started to take a drink. After pouring half the bottle into the glass Malachy would occasionally take a mouthful, but the beer would last him for the full two hours of his stay. One glass of whisky, however, would not be enough for his stay and would usually be replenished a further three or more times. This, of course, would be vey much dependent upon how lively the debate was between Malachy and the other regular patrons who visited the bar at lunch-time.

One regular customer, and the chief target of much of Malachy's most barbed statements, was John Joe McCusker. He was a small, balding, irritable man who was at least ten years younger than Malachy. About twelve inches smaller than the older man, John Joe was a sour-faced man who never smiled much in public. Malachy would tell you that John Joe was reluctant to smile because he hadn't "a bar in his grate." In layman's terms this term simply described the way in which John Joe's mouth was filled with missing, broken and rotting teeth. When John Joe spoke his words were muffled by a variety of nasal grunts and other strange sounds. Malachy was, probably, the only person in the bar who truly understood what John Joe said and, perhaps, this was the reason behind the many heated discussions that took place between the two men. Malachy, of course, considered himself to be the final arbiter on all matters regarding gaelic football. John Joe, however, was always making efforts to depose Malachy from this self-proclaimed status and he would challenge him at every possible opportunity.

It was a wet, early autumn day and Malachy had parked himself on his usual bar stool in "Healey's Bar". He had just finished his first glass of whisky and had ordered his second of the day. There was a definite chill in the air and Charlie Healey, the bar owner, had lit the fire in the old stone hearth that stood in one wall of the main bar. The large wooden logs that he had built on the fire were now well ablaze and their heat radiated throughout the entire room.

"What's wrong with your mate today?" asked Charlie.

"Who?" replied Malachy, accepting his second glass of whisky from Charlie's hands.

"McCusker," Charlie explained.

Malachy swallowed a mouthful of lager and told him, "Sure you wouldn't know what that Cowboy is up to. He has more moves in him than a bag full of weasels." Only Malachy called John Joe by the name "Cowboy" and the reason for him doing so was a mystery known only to himself. But the nickname had become so tied up with the man that many used it when referring to John Joe.

"Still, its not like McCusker to be late," Charlie Healey insisted. There was only a muffled reply from Malachy, but behind him the main bar door opened and John Joe entered, a little out of breath and a bit dishevelled by the rain that was still falling outside.

"There you go," laughed Charlie. "Speak of the Devil and he will appear."

"The Devil to you," snapped John Joe with his usual nasal grunt.

"Healey was only concerned about you," said Malachy. "He was wondering why you were late today and I was saying to him that it certainly wasn't because you were washing yourself."

"Ha, Ha! Very funny McCann," John Joe replied sarcastically.

"The usual John Joe?" Charlie asked.

"That will do, Charlie," he grunted as he removed his damp coat and hung it over the back of a chair near the blazing log fire. "There has been an awful crisis arisen," said John Joe as he returned to the bar stool beside Malachy. " That young O'Neill fellow is preparing to cut down "The Thorn" that stands proudly on his land."

Charlie returned to where John Joe was sitting, placing a bottle of "Guinness" and a glass of "Powers'" whisky in front of him. Malachy paid for the drink and John Joe raised his glass in appreciation of the gesture. He took a large mouthful of his "Guinness" and, after swallowing, wiped his lips dry with the back of his hand.

"Well, tell us what has happened Cowboy?" said Malachy impatiently.

Liftng his whisky glass John Joe took a small mouthful before he began to relate the events of that morning and his encounter with 'Young O'Neill'. John Joe explained he had been out walking with his old, half-blind dog as was his daily habit. It was as he and the dog walked along "Hill Road" that they came across young Harry O'Neill who was working in a field adjacent to the narrow country road. There was not one person in Ardshee who did not know who Harry O'Neill was. He was, in fact, the very popular captain of the Parish senior Gaelic Football team. Only three months earlier, Harry's well respected father, also known as Harry, had died of a heart attack and the young man was left to manage the farm. As was his normal practice, John Joe stopped for a moment to catch up on events with his neighbour. It was an opportunity for John Joe to ask after Harry's welfare and that of his grieving mother. Harry had told him that his mother was coping well with her loss. It was then that John Joe turned his attention to how things were on the farm.

"I am going to give up raising beef cattle now," Harry told him.

"That's a big step," remarked John Joe.

"You can't get a good price for your cattle these days," Harry replied. "What they give you for a beast now wouldn't pay the feed bill, never mind the bills from the vet."

"Aye, Harry! That's the truth of it," John Joe agreed. "But if you stop raising beef cattle, what are you going to do?"

"The first thing that I intend to do is to dig that field and plant some rapeseed. That is much more cost effective."

Although John Joe's eyes were not the best he knew there was something odd about the field to which Harry was pointing. "Is that the field with "The Thorn?" he asked.

"Aye, that's the one," Harry confirmed. "I can make more money from rapeseed than I can with cattle." John Joe's eyes showed the shock he felt at what he was hearing. "But what about "The Thorn"?" he asked nervously.

"That monstrosity and object of superstition will be the first thing to go," insisted Harry. "It has held this part of the farm back for long enough," he declared.

It was news that shocked John Joe to the very soles of his feet and he could see great disaster ahead. Never had John Joe heard such disregard for the power of the fairy folk. In fact, such a shock was it to John Joe that he was totally speechless, gazing at young Harry O'Neill in amazement and total disbelief. Even John Joe's half-blind dog had stopped struggling with his lead, sitting silently on its haunches and blankly staring up at his master.

When John Joe finally recovered his composure he explained slowly to young Harry that he could not cut down the fairy tree. "The tree belongs to the "Good People", John Joe explained. "You cannot just cut it down!"

Harry was not at all impressed by his elderly neighbour's interference and snapped at him, "This is my land, John Joe!"

"I know Harry, but -"

"But nothing! Let me tell you that no person will dictate to me what I can do with my land. No talk of fairies, or little people, or any other superstitious claptrap will stop me from doing what I want with my land."

"Don't you know you shouldn't interfere with a 'Thorn', Harry?" John Joe persisted. "Terrible catastrophes will befall you Harry should you even damage a twig on that tree."

"Bullshit!" Harry sneered. "A man of your years should know better than to spread such damn nonsense."

Angry at the response he was receiving to his pleas, John Joe snapped back at Harry O'Neill. "It is because of my age that I have been able to see so much and know the truth of what I am telling you!" But Harry was not listening to him. John Joe simply turned his back on his neighbour, and the two men now moved silently away from each other.

Malachy had listened attentively to John Joe's sad story and said nothing, just shook his head sympathetically. "That young O'Neill is a bit of a 'bollicks'," he said at last. "His father was a right sort of man and would never think about cutting down that tree."

John Joe ruefully nodded his head in agreement and took another mouthful from his glass of Guinness. "You mark my words, Cowboy. There will be no good come from young Harry cutting down that tree," Malachy added. "They say if you kill a fairy tree then death quickly follows you."

Malachy was aware of just how serious a situation Young Harry had gotten himself into and he cast his mind back to the stories surrounding "The Thorn" in O'Neill's field. He recalled, "That tree has been standing there since the days of the Celts. My father, God rest him, told me that his father, God rest him too, had told him that it was an ancient tree. In those days you could be sure that not a person would even dare to go near the tree for fear that they would disturb that local clan of fairy people."

"Harry has no regard for the 'Little People' or the mischief they can cause," John Joe told him.

"More's the pity for him," replied Malachy. "The clan at 'The Thorn' is known to be particularly vicious. You know it is only because we have cared for that tree so well that we have never had any trouble. There has been no dry cow in this Parish for many years, nor have any of our people been cursed with a changeling child."

John Joe had been steeped in the tradition of the countryside, but he had to give way to the knowledge of his friend. The folk history of the area noted that there was no record of a milk cow producing anything less than rich, creamy milk as a result of good grazing land. At the same time local calves always appeared to get a good price. Moreover, there was no story of any family in the Parish ever having to suffer the curse of a changeling child.

"The little people from around the 'Thorn' will not take kindly to Harry O'Neill destroying their home," Malachy warned. "Well, he has been warned and sure that is all any of us can do."

John Joe nodded his agreement, but added, "Surely we need to do a bit more?"

"What do you mean?" replied Malachy. "The man doesn't believe and thinks everything we are telling him is nonsense."

"Still, there must be something," urged John Joe. "I will go with you . If he cuts that tree down then the whole village could share the consequences."

The two men discussed the subject further as they took another drink or two. Meanwhile, Charlie Healey had been eavesdropping on their animated conversation, and picking up scraps of its content. It amused him to hear the two old men talk so seriously about fairies, little people, changelings and the likes. Healey, however, was clever enough to not interfere in the conversation, especially when it was between Malachy McCann and John Joe. This strategy was simply taken from his own "Do Not" list. As far as conversations in the bar are concerned, a bar-keeper does not get involved in debates between friends even when asked for their thoughts.

The discussion had come to an end and both men had decided that they should now go and personally visit the fairy tree. Together they had concluded that by acting in unison they could, perhaps, be accepted by the little people as intermediaries with young Harry O'Neill. With their hands in their trouser pockets and lit cigarettes dangling from their bottom lips the two men made their way to the field where "The Thorn" stood. The rain had ceased and with a slight stagger in their step the two pensioners considered the dangers that Harry O'Neill's action could bring about. Together, they hoped, a successful solution could be gained that would keep Harry and Ardshee safe from the anger of the "Little People".

It took the two men over twenty minutes to reached the field where the large, old and gnarled hawthorn tree stood. As they came closer to the tree John Joe began to lose his courage and decided to hold back a little. "Maybe you should go ahead and do all the talking, Malachy," suggested John Joe.

Malachy smiled to himself and nodded his head in assent. He moved toward the tree alone and began to plan in his own mind what he was going to say. Finally, as he stood before the tree, Malachy cleared his throat and began to speak under his breath. Even as he spoke Malachy's eyes scanned every nook and cranny of that twisted old tree, hoping that at least one of its inhabitants would condescend to making an appearance. "I know you hear me," he began. "You know me and all who belong to me. You also know that we hold you in the highest regard, but I must tell you that young Harry O'Neill has decided to be rid of the sacred tree that is your home. We have tried to talk him out of taking any such action and we don't want anything really bad to happen. Maybe you could act to give the boy a fright and change his mind."

John Joe watched as his friend stood before the 'Thorn' but he could not hear what he was saying. He was impressed at Malachy's courage in talking direct to the "Little People", and when his friend returned to his side he asked, "Did you speak to them?"

"I did," Malachy replied, "and they answered."

"Well, what was said?" John Joe enquired.

"They said they knew about young Harry's plans already," the old man replied and began to walk on. John Joe followed behind wanting to ask a lot more questions, but he knew he would be told all in due course.

A few days later the two old villagers walked into "Healey's Bar", after they had collected their pensions from the local Post Office. Once inside they parked their posteriors on their usual bar stools and, on this occasion, John Joe paid for the drinks.

"Did you two men hear the news about young Harry O'Neill?" asked Charlie Healey as he lifted the money from the bar.

"Never heard a word," said John Joe as he lifted his glass of "Powers" to his lips.

"We are just out of the Post Office and no one in there told us anything," Malachy added.

"Well Harry had a bad accident, yesterday," said Charlie.

"Dear God," John Joe gasped, "What happened? Is he dead?"

"For God's sake, give the man a chance to finish!" snapped Malachy.

"He's still alive and kicking," Charlie reassured them both. "He was using that digger of his to clear out a bit of drainage down by that old thorn tree." Charlie noticed the two men looking at each other with a satisfied expression on their faces, but continued with his story. "While he was operating the small bucket arm of the digger the whole thing gave way on him, and toppled into the drain. Those who found him said that he was almost drowned, saved only by the fact that some people heard his calls for help."

"He's a lucky man," John Joe interrupted.

"Lucky? Both legs are broken, he has cracked ribs, and he swallowed an entire bellyful of that stagnant drain water. The man is going to be in hospital a few weeks."

"Still lucky, I say," remarked John Joe, taking another drink.

Malachy turned to face his friend and quietly told him, "Didn't I tell you that they heard me?"

Meanwhile, Charlie Healey had finished pouring a drink for another customer and was able to return to the subject. "Do you know what the strangest and funniest thing about the whole incident was?" he asked.

"What?" replied John Joe.

"Well, when his rescuers got to him in the drain, Harry was shaking like a feather and jabbering on about crowds of "Little People". He said he had seen them dancing and celebrating on the drain's bank as he was struggling to get free from the digger."

"Must have been a shock," Malachy commented.

"Aye! Shock",Charlie laughed aloud as he moved down the bar to attend to another customer.

Malachy and John Joe turned to each other and raised their glasses to one another. "Here's to "The Little People" and our future good fortune," Malachy toasted the result.

"Amen to that," added John Joe.

THE BRIDGE

Autumn was definitely gone and the first real chills of winter had put a white covering of frost over the ground. It had been a bright day, but there was no heat from the weak sun, and the chill remained in the air. The clocks had been turned back just two weeks ago and darkness began to fall very early these days, making things all the more miserable for those who had to face the cold. Tommy was one of those people who had a very low threshold for coldness, all the more so since so much of his work took place in a cold storage plant. He didn't like the way in which the frost nipped at his nose and fingers with its icy grip, even when he wore a scarf and pair of gloves. In fact the best part of his working day was when he could sit at his desk with the small electric heater blowing warm air on his feet and lower legs.

On the ledge outside his office window a large crow landed and croaked its ugly song in the dying light of day. Over the hum of the computer Tommy could just about hear the constant dripping sound that came from a leaking gutter that ran along the edge of the factory roof. As the shadows of evening came over that wintry sky the factory workers began to leave for their various journeys home.

"You not going, Tommy?" asked Jimmy, who shared his office.

"I still have a bit to do do on these figures and I thought I would work a couple of hours extra to sort it," Tommy told him.

"OK, Tommy. Good night and I will probably see you tomorrow," Jimmy said and made his way out of the office door.

"Goodnight, mate," Tommy answered him without once lifting his eyes off the computer screen.

Within twenty minutes of Jimmy's departure the last employee left the factory and very quickly an eerie silence engulfed the entire premises. He turned the dial on the blow heater up a notch or two and prepared for a prolonged, lonely stay. Tommy took his Ipod from the top of his desk and put the earphones in-place so that he could listen to some of his favourite music while he worked. The time passed quickly, while outside the black of night had settled in.

The last few bars of Garth Brooks' "The Thunder Rolls" played through Tommy's Ipod and he began putting the finishing touches to the spreadsheet he had been working with on the computer. He switched off the Ipod and removed the earphones before he began to close down the computer. Being the last person on the premises it was Tommy's responsibility to ensure the premises were locked securely before he left for home. He lifted his coat, scarf and gloves from the back of his desk chair before putting off the lights and and locking the door behind him. It was only a few steps to the main door, where the alarm control panel was placed inside a cupboard that was built into the wall. Tommy set the alarms and left the building, closing the main door securely behind him.

Once outside the building Tommy felt the bite of the cold night air on his body and shivered. He didn't really mind having to work late, even on winter nights, but he was not looking forward to the two mile walk home in this weather. There was a definite frost dropping and a mist had begun to gather in the night air, heralding the beginning of freezing fog. Tonight the walk home along that dark, narrow, country road would feel a lot longer than usual. Usually Tommy would be sitting in the comfort and warmth of his car and listening to music.

Now he wondered why he had promised his wife to begin a fitness regime that would include walking to and from work.

Biddy was Tommy's wife and she had been complaining that he was putting on too much weight lately. She had convinced him to join her on a new diet and fitness programme, which included walking rather than driving short distances of up to three miles. Tommy did not necessarily agree with his wife on this matter and he was not so sure that the distance from home to work was a short distance; not at all "just a good stretch of the legs" as Biddy described it. Nonetheless, he was just smart enough to realise that his life would be so much easier if he simply agreed with Biddy's plans. Tommy knew from experience the agony he could expect to suffer if he opposed her will. He didn't have to be happy, he just had to do it. Now that the building was securely closed, Tommy proceeded out of the metal gate and close it behind him, barring and locking it.

Tommy shivered again as the chill of the frost bit at him, and he pulled his scarf much tighter around his neck before placing his gloved hands into the pockets of his coat. He turned to look down the long, dark, lonesome road that lay ahead of him and took a deep breath before he took the first step on his way home. The darkness was deepening rather quickly, the only light being provided by a glowing, silvery half-moon in the clear starlit sky. The eeriness of the road increased with every step Tommy took, strange shaped shadows being reflected off the tarmac the huge, almost leafless trees that ran along each side of the road. They stood like so many giant skeletons whose almost naked branches stretched out to the edge of the narrow road like spectral hands waiting for their chance to grab some unsuspecting passer-by.

As Tommy walked along the road there was a rustle of dried leaves being walked over, which mixed with the occasional crow making its raucous calls, unseen among the branches as they settled down for the night. As Tommy pulled the collar of his coat closer to his neck as protection, against the night air. He heard a fox bark in the distance, but the stillness of the night was not broken by the sound of any oncoming vehicle or person. At many parts of the road Tommy's leather soles on his shoes clicked loudly off the asphalt and echoed among the nearby trees. " This is some night to be walking this god-forsaken road," Tommy muttered to himself. He was somewhat upset that he had not stood up to Biddy's demands and refused to begin such a fitness programme just as winter had began. His step slowed as he berated himself for giving into her so easy, and it took him some time to regain a good pace again.

Not far ahead of Tommy the silvery light of the moon penetrated the mist sufficiently that he could just see the beginning of the humped back, stone bridge that marked the half-way point on the road home. He had crossed this ancient stone bridge, constructed from grey granite rocks, numerous times going to and from work. It was a cobbled, old cart track that had been repeatedly asphalted over, but still leaving it like the fabled "Rocky Road to Dublin" when you drove over it in your car. The fast flowing river over which the bridge spanned was only one of a number of similar streams that swept down from the nearby, gorse-covered hills to the Ballydunn River.

The stark ghoulish looking trees grew up beside the bridge on both banks of the stream. To a more nervous person approaching the bridge on such a cold, dark night a certain sense of fear may have given them cause to hesitate. Tommy, however, was not the nervous type. He did not believe, as many others did, the tales of ghosts and other superstitious nonsense. Seeing the bridge just ahead lifted Tommy's spirits considerably, and he felt a little warmer, but reaching this bridge always encouraged Tommy to keep trudging onward.

The dark country road had no footpath on either side of it and for safety sake Tommy always walked in the middle of the narrow road, especially in the evening darkness. By staying more to the centre of the road Tommy could avoid the larger pot-holes and the broken edges of the asphalt where it met the grass verges. In the dark a pedestrian could quite easily step into one of those pot-holes, trap their foot and cause a severe injury or fall. Furthermore, by keeping to the centre of the road the pedestrian could avoid stumbling into the puddles of ice-cold water that these pot-holes often contained.

As Tommy's footsteps brought him closer to the little, granite-stone bridge across the stream he began to notice a strange white-blue mist that was spiraling about it. The strange, thickening mist appeared to originate from the stream below the bridge, and it wound its way through the trees to the bridge itself. This was a mist that Tommy had never seen before, and it brought upon him a strange sense of fear. As the mist spiralled upward it thickened in its density, but it did not spread further outward from the bridge. Tommy tried hard to put any nervousness he felt to the back of his mind, but he could not help linking this strange mist to scenes from an old black and white movie. In those old films the grey-white mists appeared to float and drift around mysterious buildings, graveyards, and various scary backdrops. Despite his best efforts Tommy could not put his sense of nervousness to the back of his mind, and he could feel his throat beginning to dry rapidly.

Tommy's pace slowed as the beginning of the bridge got closer. There was a definite sense of fear that had begun to creep up on the man, but he could not quite put his finger on what was the cause of his fear. He did not believe in the superstitious nonsense that he had heard others speak about. Nevertheless, he could feel his heart begin to beat faster and his body begin to tremble ever so slightly. Tommy began to question himself and wondered why he should suddenly feel scared of the dark. "For God's sake this is only a fog of some kind," Tommy told himself and walked on.

He laughed quietly at his silly fears and took a deep breath before proceeding onward. As he exhaled his warm breath condensed in the cold of the night air as steam. He could feel the drops of moisture that had gathered on his moustache and he wiped it with the back of his hand. It was definitely getting colder now and he just wanted to get himself home as quickly as he could to warm himself at the blazing fire that Biddy would undoubtedly have set in the hearth. Tommy was at the bridge and only a mile away from home. In the distance he could see several dim, yellow lights that managed to shine through the darkness, reinforcing his comforting thoughts of home, Biddy and a filling meal. But, as he stepped on to the bridge the puzzling mist appeared to be gathering around him. Step by careful step Tommy moved forward, and he could feel the road rise as he approached the centre of the hump-back bridge.

Despite the density of the mist around him Tommy didn't fail to notice a slight movement in the shadows to his left. In the greyness of this mist it appeared to be an almost black, shadow. As he focused his attention upon it the shadow began to resemble the figure of a person. Tommy was certain that the figure was a female form and it seemed to be in a crouched position at the wall of the bridge. Maybe it was someone who had fallen while crossing the bridge, Tommy thought. Perhaps his approach had caused her to be frightened and she was cowering in her fear. She may have been crouching by the wall in an effort to conserve at least some of her warmth in the growing cold. Tommy was uncertain and he moved closer to the shadowy figure. He could see long grey, hair flowing from a bowed head that was resting on her arms. The figure certainly appeared to be an elderly woman who had probably stumbled on the rough road and was in need of some assistance. She, for her part, remained silent as Tommy came nearer.

Any man worth his salt could not help but pity an old woman in distress. Being the man he was Tommy was very much concerned with the poor woman's condition and moved closer to give her some assistance. His hand outstretched Tommy told her gently, "This is not a place for any person to be sitting down on such a bitter, cold night." The old lady did not stir and said nothing in reply to Tommy's enquiry. She remained motionless, holding her head in her two arms. Then, quite unexpectedly, she began to rock herself to and fro. As if in a state of some grief. "Is there anything wrong?" Tommy enquired gently so as not to frighten her. "Can I help you?" The old woman's silence continued in the face of his questions and he moved toward her until he stood by her side and looked down upon her crouching form. He began to reach down to the old woman, but something caused Tommy to stop as soon as he had started. Being so close to the woman he believed was in distress, Tommy could suddenly see that his first thoughts about her were far from the truth. She certainly was not the old lady that he had first suspected her to be.

The hair on this woman's head was sprouting in great swathes from her scalp. It swept down from her head, over her shoulders and arms, spreading out upon the cold, damp ground on which she was crouched. Tommy was completely dumbfounded by what he saw and was frozen to the spot. The long, thick and shining hair, that he had once thought was silver grey, he now saw in its true colour. It was a very pale yellow colour and it was sweeping down over a thick, grey cloak, under which she appeared to be wearing a dark green gown made of shimmering material.

The manner in which these rich looking clothes fell gracefully around the woman's body, and the way they shimmered in the misty darkness distracted Tommy. He wondered just what kind of material they were made from, for it appeared to be like nothing he had ever seen. Tommy dismissed any effort to get closer to this woman. In fact he now began to nervously step back from her, blessing himself quickly as protection from whatever evil he had stumbled into. As the figure's head moved Tommy gasped, taking a deep breath and calling out, "Sweet Jesus!"

As soon as Tommy had uttered the words, he immediately wished he had said nothing. With these words spoken the crouched woman lowered her arms from her head and turned her face towards Tommy. It was a small, round shaped face with very sharp features; a long thin nose and a chin that was pointed. Her skin was ashen pale colour, the shade of death, and her skin was both dry and heavily wrinkled, like that of a very ancient woman. Great brown freckles and age spots the size of chicken eggs covered her face and obscured some features, like her eyebrows. But this spectre's eyes were a pale, piercing blue colour, and as cold as the bright November moon that was reflected in a nearby pool of water which was beginning to ice over. She stared at Tommy with those cold eyes and they seemed to bore through him like jagged fingers of ice. They were ringed with red almost as if her eyes had been sewn into the skull with a blood red thread, which perfectly matched her crimson red lips that, as they parted, revealed her sharp and pure white teeth.

Tommy could not move. Her mesmerising, penetrating gaze had frozen him to the spot, and he could feel the cold sweat of fear ooze from every pore of his body. There was no noise but the loud thumping of his heart as it pounded heavily in his breast. His entire body began to shake with terror and panic began to take hold of his body. He wanted to scream as loud as he could when that spectral woman began to rise up from her crouched position and began to float upward. She moved as if being blown by a breeze, but there was no wind and the very sight of her convinced him that he was about to breathe his last breath. All he could do at the moment was to stand as if paralysed by this dark and terrible apparition.

She now rose up from the ground to her full height and began floating above Tommy silently swaying but never once taking its cold stare from him. She looked to him like the dead risen to life. Slowly and deliberately the apparition stretched out her arms and began to move toward Tommy, all the while using her long, bony arms to urge him to come to her. Tommy could not move, nor could he force out a scream that would alert the entire neighbourhood to the horror that was present. The fine hairs that ran along Tommy's spine now, sending shivers of anxiety through his body. He stared at the ghostly vision before him as it began to close its arms again, as if gathering itself together. When this was achieved she glided over the wall of that ancient bridge and rapidly dived down into the fast flowing, cold, dark waters of the stream. There was no splash or disturbance marking the point at which she penetrated the water's surface, but the strange mist that had surrounded her swiftly followed after her.

The ghostly apparition had gone and yet Tommy was still frozen to the same spot, unable to move a muscle. It took several minutes for his senses to return and, with them, the ability to move. He had heard tales and, yet, Tommy could not quite grasp the fact that he had encountered a "Banshee" and had lived to tell the tale. Once his senses had returned, Tommy quickly gathered himself together, mentally and physically, and he began to run for his life to the relative safety of home. As he started to run over the rest of the bridge he became suddenly surprised at just how much strength and stamina he had. He ran non-stop the entire mile from the bridge to his house, and spent little time worrying about pot-holes or rough roadside verges.

Tommy was totally exhausted by his run home from the bridge and, when he finally reached the front door of his house, he just threw himself against it. Biddy had heard the commotion and hurried to the door, which she opened to see what had caused such a noise. Tommy, still trying to catch his breath after his long run, fell into the hallway, frightening the life out of his wife. Biddy gasped as she saw her husband drop to the floor, where he lay completely still. She knelt down beside her husband and anxiously asked, "Tommy, Tommy, what has happened to you?"

Tommy could not answer because he was still trying to catch his breath and clutching at his chest.

"You are white as a sheet, Tommy! Is it your heart?" Biddy asked anxiously. Tommy, however, still could not answer and his entire body began to shake. Almost instinctively his wife seemed to know that Tommy had received a great shock and she hurried to bring a knitted throw from the sofa in the living room and placed it over his shivering body. She had closed the front door to keep the chill out of the house and continued to sit on the floor by her husband's side. It took a full twenty minutes before he could grip Biddy's hand, and through his tears told her, "I have seen the Banshee!"

It was evident that Biddy was confused by what Tommy was telling her, putting it down to shock. She helped him to get up from the floor and led him into the living room where she made him comfortable on a seat beside the blazing fire. After making him a cup of hot, sweet tea Biddy quietly asked him, "Tommy, please tell me what happened to you."

Tommy recounted the story of his journey home and the truth of his frightening encounter was discovered by Biddy the next morning. A neighbour by the name of O'Neill called at the house with sad news. His father, Hugh O'Neill, had been found dead in his bed that morning and it was presumed he had died during the night. He also reported that several family members and neighbours had heard the wailing of the Banshee, which is her call for the "Death Coach" with its headless driver to bring the poor man's soul on its last journey. "Did you hear anything?" he asked.

WITCHES OF 3 GLENSHEE

Father John Quinn was the long-time Parish Priest of Glenshee Parish, dedicated to the honour of "Our Lady of the Roses." There were none of the parishioners who did not consider Father Quinn to be a traditionally pious man, who took his ministry to the Parish very seriously. Every morning, in good weather or foul, he could be seen walking the Church grounds with his breviary. From this book he would recite his morning office before celebrating Mass in his beautiful country chapel.

There were some within the small Parish, however, who looked upon Father Quinn as a stern man, rooted in the traditionalist status of the Church and watching over the morals of his "Flock". But the majority of Father Quinn's 'flock' saw him as a very approachable and understanding cleric. Moreover, there were many who availed themselves of Father Quinn's compassionate listening skills to lighten their consciences. Most of all, however, it was the Parish Priest's habit of giving light penance after confession that endeared him to the greater majority of the parish members.

John Quinn was a priest of the old school though he was not yet sixty-three years old. It was almost thirty-five years since John had been ordained a priest and the last seven years of his ministry had been as Parish Priest in Glenshee. He could not have been described as a handsome man, but he was tall, thin-faced, and in possession of a good head of black hair that was turning grey at its edges. His voice was deep and very gravelly, described by some who heard it as being like a heavy roller being pulled over stones. Others described his voice as being deep but soft, with something of a rasp to it. It was almost as if he had a permanent infection of the throat troubling him. Yet, every Sunday he patiently read out his homily to a congregation that had nothing less than the highest respect for him as their 'Shepherd'.

The month of May, its breezes perfumed with the scent of flowers and blossom, had always been Father Quinn's favorite month of the year. In that month, which the Church dedicates to Mary, the Mother of Christ, he would conduct a special novena to the "Blessed Virgin", which was always well attended. During the month he would also lead a parish pilgrimage to Knock, and assist the "Legion of Mary" and the "Lourdes Committee" with their valuable charity work within the parish. But, unfortunately, at this time also, Father Quinn was disturbed by rumours of witchcraft. During the year there were always two or three periods of time when reports and accusations against witches and their black arts were brought before him. John Quinn never gave much of his time to such rumors and, as a priest, he was totally skeptical of such superstitions, especially the local myths that circulated in Glenshee. His skepticism was reinforced on these occasions when he saw that the main target for these rumors and accusations was Tessie O'Shea.

Tessie was, to any objective observer, an old and feeble woman of at least ninety-years, and she walked stooped-over, with the aid of a 'Blackthorn' walking stick. She attended Church as often as she was able, but she was also immersed in the folklore and legends of the countryside. There were those who would occasionally call on Tessie for the herbal charms and plant medications of old, for which she was renowned. Even the occasional young girl or boy would come to her on an evening to request a love potion to win over their true-love's heart. Naturally Old Tessie obliged all requests made of her and earned an income for herself. Father Qunn, despite the fact that Tessie was pandering to "superstitious nonsense", saw her as nothing more than a harmless old woman. In the face of this he gave no credence to the accusations of witchcraft that were often made against her, or her daughter, Sally.

Father Quinn, however, did not know all of the things for which Tessie O'Shea had become renowned. Secretly in the night young women and young wives would visit the Old Woman to request certain potions that would prevent them from conceiving. There were some who would call to obtain something that would assist their chances of successful conception. Even the hard-nosed farmers would call upon Tessie to give them 'magical' mixtures that would increase their yields from cattle, sheep, goats, pigs and land. They would ask for charms that would prevent fairies and other spirits from causing mischief among their prize assets. Tessie, of course, willingly listened to all requests for her assistance, and was often easier to pay than a vet or a doctor. Her trade would have died off many years ago if her potions, mixtures and charms that she had prepared had not been so successful in achieving the results that were needed.

The presence of Tessie and her daughter Sally was not appreciated by every inhabitant of Glenshee village. There were some who openly branded the two women as being "Servants of Satan", and condemned all those who use her evil charms and potions. Among those detractors were some of the most influential ladies in the district, and they often demanded that Father Quinn work to remove these witches from the area. When they considered that Father Quinn was not making a great enough effort to remove the witches they went above his head to the Bishop. Although neither the Bishop nor the Parish Priest could, or wanted, to do much to ensure the departure of Sally and Old Tessie, the detractors continued their campaign undaunted.

Old Tessie had lived with her daughter Sally in an old, traditionally thatched, cottage on the edge of a woodland known as "Peppers' Trees" for many years. Tessie's family were not originally from the Glenshee district, but there was no person in the district who could actually recall when they had arrived there. For most Glenshee families, therefore, Tessie O'Shea and Sally would always be considered "foreigners" or "Blow-ins." Father Quinn, at one point, considered the reports being made against Tessie were a cause for concern. As Parish Priest he called upon the old woman at her cottage to warn her about the rumours being spread about her. Under the current circumstances the priest thought it best if Tessie refrained from her habit of dispensing traditional potions and charms. But the two women seemed to remain unfazed by the Parish Priest's concerns and the suggestion that they were being identified as witches. At one stage the two women laughed aloud at the very idea that they were involved in witchcraft.

It was at this time that the attention of the people in Glenshee was distracted by terrible events among the major dairy herds in the area. For several weeks dairy farmers had become very concerned about a new phenomenon that appeared to be spreading among their herds. Several farmers had recently gone into the fields early in the morning, as was their usual habit, to bring their cows into the milking sheds. But when they went into the fields they discovered that several of their cows were lying in a pool of blood caused by a huge rip to their throats. In fact it resembled more a huge bite mark than a rip. But this large gash in their throat was the only apparent injury, and caused most farmers to blame local dogs being aloud to run wild. There were suggestions that local dog owners had failed to control their animals effectively and they had been allowed to run free in the district. There were no natural predators that could have caused such injuries, for the fox was too small an animal to bring down a fully grown cow. From the evidence the blame could only be put upon a large dog or cat-like animal. The strangest fact, perhaps, concerning all the deaths was that none of the cattle had been killed for food.

Each cow was found with a deep bite wound to the throat, while the rest of the animal was left untouched by its attacker. Joe Hagan, at the outer edge of the district, loudly argued against any domestic animal, cat or dog, being responsible for the attacks. Joe told his neighbors and others that he had gone out to his cattle an hour earlier one morning. He wanted to finish early to allow him to attend a local auction, where he could purchase replacements for those animals he had lost to the mysterious beast. In the first bright rays of that morning Joe had seen yet another cow lying dead on the ground, and his eyes caught sight of a huge black, cat-like animal that ran swiftly into a hedgerow before disappearing from view.

From the beginning of the macabre deaths there had been rumblings of evil witchcraft being behind the mystery. When Joe related what he had seen the rumblings turned to bitter accusations that witches were at their work. Many suggested that the large, black cat-like animal was nothing less than a witch's familiar, or animal spirit. "Utter nonsense," Father Quinn insisted. Even after Joe O'Hagan had collapsed at the front door of his farmhouse, the priest maintained his stand against superstitions.

Joe O'Hagan's doctor was very puzzled by his collapse. He was not a man who had experienced a lot of illness in his lifetime, but the doctor thought the collapse could have been caused by a sudden spike in his blood pressure. This spike, the doctor believed, had been caused by stress about the mysterious destruction of so many cattle, combined with exhaustion from overwork. Joe, keen to stay on his farm, refused to follow the doctor's advice and stay in hospital for a few days to be checked out medically. He did, however, agree to spend at least all of the following week in his bed, resting. Joe's wife had been assured that if Joe did all that was asked of him then he would recover fully from the collapse.

Father Quinn had visited Joe that same day and had heard the assurances the doctor had given Mrs. O'Hagan. He said evening Mass in the church and included Joe in the "Prayers of the Faithful," asking the congregation to pray for Joe's full recovery. After supper he stood before the large crucifix in the living room of the parochial house praying his "compline", or night prayers from his breviary. He was about half-way through these prayers when he was disturbed by loud, rapid knocking at the front door of the house. He didn't like his time at prayer interrupted, but he closed his breviary and set it down upon a nearby chair seat. The priest marched smartly to the front door and opened it. He was surprised to see, standing on the doorstep, Joe O'Hagan's son, Martin. "Martin?" he greeted the visitor. "It's late for you to be out and about, but come in."

The young man standing on the door step was panting as he held a tight grip on the bicycle at his side. " Please Father, I have been sent to fetch you. It's urgent! Will you come?"

Father Quinn saw the panic in the eyes of the young man and was quite concerned. " In the name of God Martin, what has happened?"

"It's my Da, Father" Martin told him, tearfully shaking his head as he spoke. "He's took a terrible turn for the worse, Father. He needs you!"

"My car is open, Martin. Get yourself into it and I will be with you in a moment. Just as soon as I gather up my things,"

As Father Quinn hurried back into the house the young man left his bicycle up against the wall of the house and made his way to the passenger side of the car. Just a few moments later the Parish Priest had gathered up everything he needed and he rushed out of the door, closing it firmly behind him. He hurried to his car and quickly climbed into the driver's seat beside Martin, who had already secured his seat-belt. Although the darkness of the night was deepened by the lack of moonlight it had remained dry and was ideal for the drive to O'Hagan's farm. Turning on the ignition and the car's lights Father Quinn drove the car out of the Parochial House grounds and on to the main road. With the car's headlights at full beam he drove speedily along the narrow country roads to O'Hagan's farm. Martin, in the front passenger's seat, had some reason to feel genuinely anxious about his own safety in the car. But, despite his concerns, Martin could hardly wait to get back home and check just how his father was getting on.

A very few minutes after leaving the Parochial House, Father John pulled into the main yard of O'Hagan's farm, the wheels spinning in the mixture of manure and mud that had been deposited there. But the priest managed to park his car safely, much to Martin's relief. Indeed Martin was the first to undo his seat-belt and exit the car within a second or two of it stopping. Father Quinn followed close behind and as he entered the house he met Martin's younger sister, who told him, "My Mother's in the bedroom with Dad. It's not looking good, Father." Her eyes were red and swollen from the tears that she had shed in the hours since her father's collapse.

The priest gave his coat to the young girl at the front door and followed Martin into the bedroom where Mrs. O'Hagan watched over the ailing body of her husband. Joe O'Hagan, normally a hale and hearty fellow lay in that bed, a pale yellow pallor on his skin, and his eyes sunk into his head. Mrs. O'Hagan silently mopped up the cold sweat that had begun to cover the dying man's face and she whispered softly to Joe. Joe, for his part, could not answer his wife's whispers to him. His breathing grew shallow and it was as if the last embers of life were about to be extinguished. Father Quinn could see that time was fast running out and he placed the purple stole around his neck. Opening his breviary the priest began the service for "anointing the sick" to which Martin and his mother spoke the responses.

As the hours passed Joe's breathing grew shallower. Martin had been sent to a neighbour's house to telephone the doctor to see if anything more could be done, even at this late stage. The doctor, however, knew that he could do nothing more for the dying man, and informed the family that now it was simply a waiting game. He was, of course, correct in his prognosis. Just after two o'clock in the morning Joe O'Hagan took one last deep breath and expired. As that last breath was expelled from the body there was a sound, almost a rattle from the man's throat, which confirmed that his soul had now departed the body. The Parish Priest stood up and, reaching over the body, he closed the dead man's eyes while giving him the final blessing. Mrs. O'Hagan, burst into tears and, rising from Joe's bedside, rushed out of the bedroom into the arms of her children. Father Quinn, meanwhile, gently lifted Joe's head from the pillows, removing them to allow the head to rest fully horizontal on the mattress. He then called the family back into the bedroom, where they gathered around the death-bed to join in the rosary being prayed for the happy repose of Joe's soul.

It was well after three o'clock in the morning when the Parish priest left the house. Before he left he took Martin to one side and told him, "It's time for me to go now and, maybe, I will get a couple of hours rest before I say morning Mass. I will call again in the morning before lunch and we can take things from there."

"That's fine Father. I could go with you and bring home my bicycle," Martin suggested.

Father Quinn, however, thought that the place for Martin to be at this time was home. He told him gently, "You should leave that until tomorrow, Martin. Your mother and sister need you now, for there will be much to do and arrange over the next twenty-four hours."

Martin fully appreciated the priests advice and retrieved his coat. As Father Quinn walked out of the front door, the first rays of dawn's light were beginning to illuminate the sky above the hills in the east. The priest yawned, giving way to his tiredness, as he walked over to his parked car and climbed into the driver's seat. There was a slight mizzle of rain falling as he started the car engine, and switched on the windscreen wipers. As he released the handbrake, Father Quinn steered the car out of the farmyard into the long farm lane that ran between two of Joe O'Hagan's fields. It was a very bumpy ride down this long lane until it finally came to the main road to Glenshee. At this junction, Father Quinn turned the car left and drove on toward the village.

The Parish Priest was looking forward to getting home and back into his bed, even if it was only for an hour. He just wanted to close his tired eyes and catch up on at least some of the sleep he had missed. But, he drove slowly, worried that tiredness might make him careless. At the same time the priest admired the way the morning light spread across the countryside, enhancing all the natural colors and hues of the district. He loved the beauty which nature always exhibited and he constantly strove to find ways in which he could include this beauty in his homilies. As he was considering this question the engine began to 'cough' and the car spluttered to a stop. He turned his eyes heavenward and was ready to swear aloud, but he had second thoughts and chose to say a quiet prayer instead. There was only another mile or so to the Parochial House, but he no longer had need to hurry. Thankfully the car had free-wheeled to the side of the road and Father Quinn sat in the driver's seat reading his breviary, which he had taken from the passenger seat.

As he neared the end of his "Morning Office", Father Quinn decided he would walk to the Parochial House. He was feeling much calmer now and, locking the car, he began to walk toward Glenshee in a smart, but leisurely fashion. After walking several yards along the road he noticed a large, white horse approach the wooden fence that ran adjacent to the road. It was a tall, statuesque animal and Father Quinn fought the temptation to go to the fence and admire this beautiful steed. He realized that if he was to get home, shower and breakfast before Mass, he had little time to stop and admire this horse. He walked on a little further and began to notice that this horse was acting in a very strange manner. It was shaking its head, kicking his hind legs in the air, and banging its body against the wooden fence that stood between it and the road. Father Quinn became concerned that the horse would do itself some severe injury, and he began to approach it slowly. He spoke soothingly to the horse to calm it, but as he drew nearer he could see that the horse's entire body trembled and was sweating profusely.

The Parish Priest's presence didn't do much to ease the stress that the horse appeared to be feeling, and he wondered what more he could do. Father Quinn had little hands-on experience of horses, but he was certain that something had startled the animal. It was very frightened and something must have caused it to become so disturbed. With nervous courage the priest climbed over the wooden fence and continued to talk in soothing tones to the horse, trying to calm its fears. He managed to get close enough to the horse to gently take hold of its neck and softly pat it with his hand. As he did this, however, he noticed something very strange near the hedge, that grew thickly against the fence, a little further along the road. For a moment he rubbed his eyes, for he could not quite believe what he was seeing. At first he thought that the loss of sleep was catching up with him, but he soon felt a great sense of fear filling his body. Ahead of him, and coming towards him, was what appeared to be a large, black feline creature. It filled in every way the description of the animal seen by

Joe O'Hagan and now it was making its way toward Father Quinn silently, step by careful step.

Both horrified and frightened by the monstrous feline that approached, Father Quinn held his nerve and turned to his faith for help. He was assured by that faith he held so dear that with God on his side there was nothing in the world for him to fear. The priest stood solidly at the side of the trembling horse and stared down at the huge, black creature, that bared its teeth as it came to a halt just a few yards ahead. In the bright, early, morning sunlight the creature's black fur glistened, and its evil green eyes never moved away from its intended prey. Father Quinn could see that there was blood dripping from the side of the creature's mouth, indicating to him that it had already killed that night. As he stared at the animal he became more certain that this creature was not an inhabitant of this world and, courageously, he called out to it, "Who are you, Demon?"

There was no reply from the creature, but the priest continued. "Who are you, Demon? What foul business are you about this fine morning?"

There was still no reply from the monster, but it raised its back, gave a fierce, unearthly growl and made ready as if to pounce. "Go in the name of God, I say," declared the priest in a shaking voice. "There is no place for Satan's servants here."

Again he was answered by a fierce roar from the throat of this diabolical creature. In response the priest grasped the cross on the rosary beads in his pocket. He took out the beads and brandished the crucifix before the beast crying out, "In the name of Jesus Christ I demand that you go from this place!"

The monstrous beast roared even louder than before and began to run toward the priest. Only a few feet away it launched itself into the air with a frightening scream, causing Father Quinn to step to one side to avoid its huge claws and teeth. It was a narrow escape for the priest whose rosary beads had been swept from his hand by the sharp claws. The priest steadied himself again and heard yet another unearthly scream from behind him. As he turned he saw the huge, black monster lying prostate on the ground and was suddenly surprised by a bright flash. This was quickly followed by a huge cloud of thick, black smoke that temporarily hid the creature from view. As the cloud of dense smoke began to clear, however, the priest was completely dumbstruck by what he saw on the ground before him. Once again he had to call into question what his eyes were telling him. He began, suddenly, to feel very dizzy and the world about him began spinning, causing his mind to be filled with a multitude of colours. Father Quinn fell to the ground, where he lay motionless for what seemed only a few minutes before his senses began to return to him. He looked in the direction where the beast had landed and saw that it had completely vanished. It was, as he had first seen after the smoke had cleared, the body of Tessie O'Shea lying where the monster had been. She was the elderly woman who had so often been reported to him as a witch. Now she lay, writhing in agony and groaning so piteously. "Tessie, Tessie, what has become of you?" he asked as he carefully approached her.

"Father, Father can you save me?" she cried out. "The evil one is ready to drag me down to him!"

The priest could say nothing, despite the old woman's pleas. He was not prepared for events such as this and could only watch as her pain increased. As she writhed in agony her body twisted and contorted into a thousand impossible positions. Tessie's body began then to swell to an incredible size. Her eyes stared at him like daggers and she uttered terrible curses toward him, spitting them out with every ounce of bile she could muster. Finally her writhing and hissing ceased as her eyes closed in death. He confirmed to himself that she had expired and he hurried to the Parochial House, from where he rang the appropriate people, informing them of what had happened to old Tessie.

There was some doubt about the priest's story, but the veracity of the Parish Priest was beyond question. The old woman's remains were removed from the field and, eventually, brought to the small cottage at "Pepper's Trees," where she had lived. She had, throughout her life, professed to be Catholic, but it was decided her occult activities could not allow her to be buried in sanctified ground. She was interred, instead, in an unmarked grave, beside a cross-roads that would always be known as "Tessie's Cross". Meanwhile, Sally, Tessie's daughter disappeared from the district on the eve of her mother's burial and no trace of her was ever found. The old cottage in which the two women had lived was mysteriously burned to the ground one night, a short time after Tessie was buried. No person was ever charged with committing the arson, and a wall of silence was built up around the event.

MARTH'S TALE

Glenshee was just a quiet village, quietly nestling among the scenic hills in the south-east of Ireland, and was not a large or populous place. Typical of an Irish country village, Glenshee had only a small population of a few hundred souls. The two public houses, a Church, a Post Office, and several small shops served the needs of these people very adequately. The hardware store in Glenshee had a particularly profitable relationship with the local farming community, and the owner served as the only undertaker in the district.

Housing in the village is divided over two areas. In the centre of Glenshee stand some eight to ten small, traditional cottages that, for the most part, are owned by families who have lived in the village for many generations. The second, and most populous area, lies at the southern edge of the village and consists of twenty-five modern houses, built by the local council. These are largely occupied by workers employed in the local creamery and cheese processing factory, which had been established just outside the village boundary.

The main bulk of Glenshee's population, however, lives outside the village on the various farms spread throughout the district. It could be said that Glenshee's very existence depended upon the farming community, since most of the population is employed directly or indirectly in this particular industry. Naturally in such a society, the wealthiest had the most influence and, in Glenshee, the undisputed "Queen Bee" was Martha Toland. Her influence was based solely on the fact that she owned the Post Office and the local supermarket.

To state that Martha Toland was a self-made woman, who had risen to the top through her own work, would be erroneous. She was indeed the owner of two very profitable local businesses, but to say she actually operated them would be stretching the truth. In reality Martha spent the majority of her time in her large, comfortable bed nursing one imaginary illness or another. The term "Physical Exertion" was anathema to Martha and she regularly excused herself from anything that even approached physical exertion by declaring, "I'm not one bit well." This was her signal to immediately retire to her large, four-poster bed, maybe for several weeks at a time, and expect everyone to dance to her attention.

It had not always been this way with Martha. When a young woman of eighteen years she was known for her exceptional good looks and her joy of dancing. Her beauty and lively personality caused Martha to become an object of desire for many young men in the district. Martha, however, had her own plans for her future and she, therefore, set her cap for Sean Cavan, the son of the wealthiest farmer in the area.

Martha may have not known what it was like to actually love another person, but the prospect of marrying a rich man was much more attractive to her. She made her move one night at a parish dance and he, in his naiveté, fell for her hook, line and sinker. Martha knew what men needed and she laid her snare well. Sean simply fell into her arms and into her snare. They rolled together in the haystack, and Martha submitted herself to his every desire, finally pulling the door to the trap shut.

It was, of course, the honey-trap strategy she employed and, in due course, Martha announced that she was pregnant. At the time of the announcement she was not pregnant, but she ensured that they enjoyed each others company enough times to make certain that she did become pregnant. Sean, being the gentleman that he was, believed Martha from the very beginning, stood by the girl, and married her. Only three months after the wedding Martha gave birth to a fine, healthy son whom she and Sean called Desmond, though preferred to call him "Dessie". Almost immediately after leaving the maternity home with her newborn son a change overcame her. She was no longer the lively young woman she had been and began to suffer the first of her debilitating illnesses, for which no real evidence could be found. From that time Martha led her young husband a 'merry dance', which many would later say brought about Sean's early demise.

Sadly, although the rightful heir to the Cavan estate, Sean was destined never to enjoy his inheritance because he pre-deceased his parents. The reason for his early death, however, was laid at the door of Martha because, they said, he wore himself down from taking care of his wife and child. It was Sean who fed, washed and cared for his son as Martha took to her bed with her mystery illness. Sean took responsibility for cooking and serving his wife's meals while she lay in her bed. He continued to work on the farm from the early hours of the morning until late at night. At the same time he took care of their home, while dancing attention to Martha's every request.

When Sean passed away many of his friends and relatives began to point the finger at Martha. The young farmer, they alleged, ran himself into the ground working all day, every day, and then rushing about answering his wife's every need. It was Sean's heart that gave in and he died while attaching a baler to the back of his tractor. The tragedy left Martha a young widow with a son and only enough insurance money to take care of the funeral. Her in-laws, because they blamed Martha for Sean's death, granted her nothing. With Sean's departure it looked like Martha's days of ease and money had come to an abrupt end.

Martha, however, had other plans. She was still relatively young and had successfully maintained her fine figure and her attractiveness to men. There was, of course, the required period of mourning to be observed before she could effectively put herself back in the marketplace. But Martha had never been one to observe traditional customs and, furthermore, black was not a color that flattered her. In her mind twelve months was too long a period of time to be out of the marketplace if she was to 'net' herself a man, and a lifestyle that suited her.

Not being prepared to mourn her husband's death for twelve months was a decision that was helped by the fact that one businessman in the village had always shown a healthy interest in her. Whenever she crossed this man's path he would always give her a sly wink of his eye and a warm, welcoming smile. Martha was fully aware that this man would never be considered handsome, in the mold of "Robert Redford" or "Johnny Depp", but he had certain attractive assets. For a start he had all his own teeth and a head of thick, well-groomed hair. The man's greatest asset, as far as Martha was concerned was that he owned and operated the village Post Office and Supermarket. In fact the only negative mark against the man that Martha could see was that he was at least twenty years older than her.

The size of Conn Riley's bank balance more than compensated for any negatives that he may have had in Martha's mind. At the same time Martha was aware that Conn's immediate past had not been a happy one and he might just be susceptible to her charms. His previous wife, Emma, was well-known in the village to have been a woman with a vicious, poisonous tongue. It was also rumored that Emma ordered her compliant husband around like any lapdog. Martha had also heard that Conn had never looked happier than he did on that day when Emma was finally laid to rest in the parish graveyard.

Martha may have been obliged by convention to conform to wearing traditional black during her period of mourning, but she was determined the color would enhance rather than detract from her attractiveness. On every occasion that she could find to visit the Post Office, Martha would make sure that she dressed in her most fashionable clothes. Moreover, since Martha had made her decision to become Conn's second wife, she had found more and more occasions to go into the Supermarket. It did not go unnoticed that every time Martha met Conn she always had a broad and inviting smile for him.

There was nothing Martha enjoyed more than getting compliments from a man and she encouraged more by unashamedly, flirting playfully with Conn. With a shy air about her she would often reply, "Oh, Mr Riley! Thank you for your kind remarks."

"It's not kindness," Conn would insist, "but the truth."

"Thank you again," Martha would giggle like a young immature woman.

Conn would blush a little and assure Martha, "You are like a breath of fresh air in my life."

"Now you're teasing," Martha would declare and leave the man with his heart fluttering with happiness.

It was Martha that was doing all the teasing, and Conn didn't care because he enjoyed every minute of the attention that she gave him. Conn could honestly state that his late wife, Emma, had never teased him playfully or smiled enticingly at him. He could never recollect an occasion when Emma made a suggestive invitation with an expression of her eyes or a pout of her lips. Every time Martha left the shops he would stare after her for several moments as if in a daydream, as he imagined passionately kissing her beautiful, soft and full lips. As the days moved into weeks and the weeks into months Martha gradually opened the door to Conn's heart. Finally, she decided to play her final card to capture that heart and close the door behind her.

Martha had been wearing widow's black for six months and had decided that all criteria expected of a grieving widow had been fulfilled. Sean had been a good man and a caring husband, but when he passed away Martha had been left with very little support. During those six months of mourning Martha had been cultivating the passions of Conn Riley and, she had decided, the time had come to put her plans into action. He was painfully shy and if she was to wait for him to make the first move she would be an old maid.

Cursing the shyness of the man, Martha devised a strategy that would use all her wiles to win through to her final goal; namely to become the second Mrs. Conn Riley. The Christmas season brought with it the ideal opportunity for Martha to launch her plan and, with this in mind, she went to Riley's shop to buy her usual daily newspaper. It was a cold, crisp winter morning and the frost crunched under foot. As Martha entered the shop she immediately noticed Conn standing behind the cash register, and she greeted him warmly. Conn, as always, smiled at her and answered her greeting with one of his own. Out of her pocket Martha took sufficient coins to pay Mr. Riley. It was at this moment that Martha decided to seize her chance. "I am so upset, Conn," she told him, with a sad tone in her voice, which immediately attracted Conn's sympathetic ear.

"What ever is the matter, Martha?" Conn asked her and came out to her from behind the counter. "Can I help?"

"No Mr. Riley," she replied trying to force a smile. "Pay me no mind" she told him. "I am just being a very silly woman." She managed to force a smile from her lips, but also kept a certain tone of despair in her voice.

Conn took Martha's arm gently and brought her to a seat in a more private area of the shop. Once he had Martha seated comfortably he quietly asked, "Please tell me what is wrong."

"Honestly, it's not important," she insisted.

"They say a problem shared is a problem halved."

"Its Joe Dolan," Martha said finally.

"What has he done?" Conn asked, a note of anger creeping into his voice.

Martha laughed,"Joe Dolan, the singer."

"The singer?" Conn repeated, feeling rather embarassed.

"He's my favorite singer," Martha told him. "He is playing in Ballymagarrett on Saturday night and I won't be able to see him."

"But, why not?" he asked.

Martha looked up at Conn with a sorrowful look in his face. "Sean would have taken me, God rest him," she sighed. "Now I have no one who will escort me to the dance," Martha spoke quietly but pouted her lips in an attractive and seductive manner.

"Sure I am the man for the job," volunteered Conn, eagerly seizing his opportunity. "I will take you to the dance on Saturday night," he offered and put his arm around her in a comforting manner.

Martha pressed herself closer into Conn, putting her face closer to his and whispered seductively, "Call for me at eight?"

"It's a date," Conn whispered back. There was an excitement in his voice as he debated whether or not he should kiss her now. He decided against kissing her but for Conn it was already too late. Martha had set the trap for him and now, like a blind man falling from a cliff, he was falling into that trap without seeing what lay ahead.

Just over three months after this first date, less than a year after Sean's untimely death, Martha and Conn Riley married each other during a nuptial mass celebrated by the Parish Priest in St. Kevin's Church. Their honeymoon was nothing very special, just a week-end in Dublin and then back to Glenshee for the shops opening on Monday morning. On that very same day Martha moved Dessie and herself into the living area above the Post Office, where Conn lived. It suited Martha's needs much better than the house she rented in the estate. Moreover, as the wife of the man who operated two successful businesses, she had a new position in the village that needed to be upheld. From the moment that Martha moved in Conn hadn't a word to say when it came to his own home or business.

Conn had successfully operated his businesses for several years, but he was a man who did not like confrontation. Henceforth, Conn operated the businesses and took care of the home, in name only. It was Martha who made all the decisions and ensured that Conn carried them out. Furthermore, within weeks of their honeymoon ending, Martha's mysterious illnesses returned to plague her life and, once again, the bed became her favorite refuge from physical activity. In that bed she slept alone and was waited on hand and foot by both her son and her husband. On occasion some of the employees were sent to act as servants.

Unfortunately for Conn he was much older and less of a physical specimen of manhood than Sean Cavan. He was not fit enough to undertake the stresses and strains of being married to Martha, and he lasted less than three years after his marriage. Unlike her marriage to Sean, however, Martha inherited everything and, almost overnight, she became a very wealthy single lady. Dessie inherited nothing. He was Martha's child but she had not given Conn any children to love and care for.

Dessie Cavan grew up to be nothing more than a slave to his mother, who continued to play on her phantom illnesses. But, Dessie inherited much of his mother's good looks and much of his father's work ethic. He grew into a very handsome hard working young man who won the hearts of many of the young, single ladies in the district.

In his late teens one particular young lady called Colleen made her way into his heart. He fell so much in love with the young girl that he began to spend all of his leisure time, whatever little there was of it, in her company. When Martha discovered that her son was dating this young lady she had a sudden, suspicious collapse in the Post Office, after which she went to bed complaining about her heart.

As Martha took to her sick-bed, Dessie was left to operate the Post Office and Supermarket on his own. The administration and stock work was overwhelming but Martha would not permit him to increase staff, even on a temporary basis. Of course, as well as the extra work in the business, Dessie was expected to look after Martha's every need. As a result young Dessie found that he had less and less time to spend with his girlfriend. Although this was exactly what Martha had planned yet, on every possible occasion, she persisted in confronting her son about his relationship with a local girl. Martha told Dessie, that Colleen was not good enough for him, as he would inherit everything when her time came. "She's nothing more than a 'Jam Tramper' and will bring you nothing!" she would scream at him. "There are better placed ladies out there for you!"

Dessie knew his own mind, however, and angrily disagreed with his mother's opinion. But, when he would remonstrate with her she would clasp her chest and claim that she was experiencing severe pain in her heart. Naturally, being a caring person, Dessie had no wish to cause his mother any more pain or discomfort, and he would cease the argument. Nevertheless, the young man began to realize that the time had come in his own life when he needed to be able to make his own choices in life without interference from his mother. In the future he had planned for himself Dessie wanted to take Colleen as his wife. Martha, he knew, would do everything in her power to ensure that this would not happen. Dessie had been told, ever since he was a child, that his chief responsibility was to look after his mother and do all he could for her.

It was a summer's day when a strangely worded telegram arrived at the Post Office, addressed to "Mrs. Martha Riley". It was given to Martha immediately and she opened it to see who had sent it. The news it contained greatly interested her - "Dear Martha," it began. "I am your late husband's spinster aunt. Sadly, I am now confined to bed with a terminal disease and would be glad of your assistance. Please come to visit me soon and help me sort out my affairs. I wish to ensure that all I have is passed on to my dear nephew's family." This, of course, was all good news to Martha, because it promised her even more riches. She read on, "I will expect you next Friday morning and we can spend the week-end together. Perhaps, now is a good time for us to get to know each before it is too late for me."

The thought of enriching herself further had a miraculous affect on Martha's condition. Her current illness disappeared in moments and she jumped out of her sick bed. She had only two days of preparation if she was going to make the journey to Dublin, and she wanted to look her very best when meeting Conn Riley's aunt. She pulled her best suitcase down from above the wardrobe, opened it, and began to select a range of clothes to pack into it. Martha also called downstairs to Dessie, who was in the Post Office, and asked him to attend to her. When Dessie came into the room he was surprised to see his mother out of bed and frenziedly working to pack a large suitcase.

"What's happening?" he asked.

"I am going to Dublin on Friday morning and will be staying the week-end with Conn's aunt," Martha told him.

"Are you well enough to take on such a journey?" Dessie inquired.

Martha was not used to having her decisions questioned and she turned angrily on her son, snapping, "Do you think I would be going to Dublin if I was not fit enough for the journey?"

"Of course not," apologized Dessie.

"Good. All you have to do is look after the business while I'm away. I will be back on Monday morning," She told him.

"But, why are you going in the first place?"

That is none of your business," Martha bluntly told him. "Just you do what you are told and keep your distance from that Colleen girl! Understand?"

"Of course", replied Dessie, knowing in himself that keeping away from Colleen was not on his agenda.

Martha got out of bed bright and early on Friday morning to finish her preparations before leaving for Dublin. Although she ate breakfast with her son, she reused to enlighten him any further on her decision to go to the city. Dessie, from previous experience, knew that it was for him not to press the point. Instead, after breakfast, Dessie gathered his mother's bags and placed them in the back seat of her car. "Remember Dessie, no Colleen. I will be back on Monday lunchtime and we will go over the business figures then," she told him abruptly.

Martha climbed into the driver's seat of her car and turned the ignition key. Closing her seat belt she put the car into first gear and pulled away from the kerbside. The wheels spun a little as she pressed her foot down on the accelerator and yet, for someone who drove as badly as Martha did, it wasn't a bad get away. Dessie returned to the Post Office and began to prepare the shops for opening.

Friday morning always started slowly in Glenshee and only got busy when the creamery closed at one-thirty in the afternoon. The supermarket always had a regular group of customers who called for their daily papers, cigarettes, milk and other necessities. But, the Post Office had its busiest day on a Monday when the pensions were paid out. It was a morning for a little bit of peace and quiet, and Dessie decided that he would man the Post office.

As Dessie finished some book-work he noticed a white police car pull up at the kerbside outside the Post Office. The blue light on the car roof was flashing and Dessie watched as two uniformed police constables got out of the car. They came to the door of the Post Office, causing Dessie to wonder why they would be calling with him so early on a Friday morning. They came through the door and made their way to the counter. "Mr. Cavan?" the taller of the two policemen asked.

"Yes, that's me," Dessie replied, with a puzzled expression on his face.

"You are the son of Mrs. Martha Riley?"

"Yes," answered Dessie with a degree of concern in his voice. "Is there something wrong?"

"We are sorry, Mr. Cavan but we have some bad news to tell you," the constable said, removing his hat.

"Bad News? What's happened?"

"Your mother has been involved in a car accident this morning, and unfortunately she did not survive," Dessie was informed

Dessie suddenly felt dizzy and sat down on a nearby chair to help regain his composure. "Do you know what happened?"

"Mr Cavan, the cause of the accident has not yet been determined but it is likely your mother took a severe heart attack while driving. Her car appears to have veered off the road and hit a large tree at full speed. There is every probability that your mother knew very little about it and was killed almost immediately."

To this day, those who remember the event, say that they had never seen Dessie Cavan looking so fit and healthy as he did on the day Martha was buried. Almost the entire village of Glenshee attended the funeral and watched as she was placed in the same grave as her late husband, Conn. With the passing of Martha, Dessie became a wealthy young man in his own right. Fortunately he had inherited the work ethic of his father Sean and, a month after burying his mother, Dessie married Colleen. Thereafter, this young and industrious couple prospered well and raised four beautiful, healthy children in the Post Office. Every Sunday, after Mass, Dessie and his family would place a bunch of fresh flowers on his Mother's grave. There are those in the village who would tell you that on these visits to the graveyard Dessie always had a knowing smile on his face as he read the epitaph he had specially commissioned for his Mother's headstone: "She always said she was not one bit well."

MISTRESS

"The Abbey" stood on a small hill, at the end of a half-mile dirt track that linked the old, dilapidated country house to the main "Tirowen Road". In the village that was nearby this large, abandoned, building had built up a local reputation as a place of ghosts and evil spirits. Even small children were warned by concerned parents that they should never go near that place at any time, especially at night. All around the property there were signs telling people, "Danger! Keep Out!"; "Private Property, Keep Out!"; "No Trespassing!" and "No Entry at Any Time!"

"The Abbey" had not always been a ruin. At one time it had been owned by the wealthy and influential "Taylor" family, whose right to the land had been established during the "Williamite Wars" of the late seventeenth century. They, it was told, held ownership of large areas of fertile farming land, which they rented out to tenants to gather an income for themselves. In those far off days "The Abbey" was a house that was full of life, laughter and joy. The "Taylor Family" and their successors enjoyed the good life and hosted dinner-parties and balls for all the gentry in the area. It attracted the company of many of the County and Provincial leading lights of genteel society. There are many rumours that are connected to the fall of this once great house. Stories vary as to why the house was finally abandoned and fell to ruin. In the "Ardcraig" area, however, everyone will tell you that "The Abbey" is a building that has been cursed by terrible circumstances, in which the spirits of the dead wreaked their revenge upon the living.

Jonathan Taylor was the last of the "Taylor Family" to own the property and he had inherited it after both his parents tragically died at sea on their way home from London. The size of his inheritance made Jonathan a wealthy young man and, probably, the most eligible bachelor in the entire Province. Every lady of the landed gentry now looked upon young Jonathan Taylor as a most suitable husband for their single daughters. After a suitable period of mourning for his parents Jonathan found himself inundated with invitations to visit some of the best houses in the country. But, for these eager ladies, it was already too late because Jonathan had "set his cap" for one particular young lady. This target for Jonathan's love was the only daughter of a local gentleman farmer whose land lay adjacent the "Taylor Estate." She was a beautiful, gently spoken young lady with skin as clear and smooth as pure porcelain. Jonathan loved the way her long, fair and silken hair would fall down, flowing softly over her shoulders. Even the shortest, innocent glance from her piercing blue eyes would set Jonathan's heart racing with excitement. As he watched the target of his love move gracefully before him, he could feel his heart pound in his breast. It pounded so hard that he was almost certain that it would burst out of his body at any minute.

Unfortunately for Jonathan he had competition in his pursuit of Alison Stuart. There were, in fact, several well-placed young bachelors who were eager to bring Alison to their bridal bed. To date, however, Alison had shown no real inclination to give up her single life, and settle down to the life of a married lady. This, at least, was the "state of play" until Alison's father invited the young Mr. Taylor to a business luncheon at his home. On that day Jonathan and Alison were introduced to each other, formally, and the young lady was greatly impressed by the handsome, well-mannered, young gentleman.

Jonathan may have been young, handsome, rich and popular but he was also a very shy person. He was, as far as young ladies were concerned, a complete novice in developing relationships. Despite his fondness for Alison and her fondness for him, very little headway was being made between the two of them. As the weeks passed Alison became quite concerned about whether or not Jonathan would ask for her hand in marriage. Anxiously she turned to her loving, and influential, father, for his assistance in the matter. Sir Robert Stuart loved his beautiful daughter and wanted only what was best for her. Fortunately he was very much in favor of his daughter marrying the dashing young Jonathan Taylor and uniting their two families.

In the end Sir Robert discovered that Jonathan did not need much persuasion to ask him for Alison's hand in marriage. Within a very few months the young couple were married and the occasion was celebrated with a great dinner and ball to which all the leaders of local society were invited. There was much comment on how happy the young couple appeared to be. The next morning the newly wedded couple set off on their honeymoon, which would take them to Dublin and London. Several weeks later they returned to "The Abbey" at Ardcraig, where Alison threw herself wholeheartedly into her new position as "Lady of the Manor". Life for them both could not have been better and they were not embarrassed to show others how much in love they were. Alison with her beauty, gentility and kindness quickly won over Jonathan's tenant farmers and the people of Ardcraig village. Much to her joy, only a few months into the marriage, Alison was able to tell her husband that they were expecting their first child. Both were overjoyed and felt that their lives were now fulfilled.

The cold, ice-laden, winds of winter blew heavily across the land the night Alison went into labor. The doctor was sent for, but the bad weather greatly delayed their arrival at "The Abbey". While examining the pain ridden Alison the doctor came to the conclusion that there was nothing that he could do for Jonathan's young wife. Complications set in and the devastated young husband could only hold his beloved wife's hand as she passed away. In that moment it was as if the light in his life had been extinguished. Alison and his unborn child were both gone, leaving him alone in his room listening to the bitter, cold winds of winter blow against the windows of his house. Jonathan, however, could feel nothing. It was as if his body had been numbed by the tragedy he had witnessed.

The snowdrops and flowering daffodils were welcomed in the Spring as they danced in the soft breezes that blew from the hills. Even in the natural beauty that shone all around "The Abbey" it remained a cold and dark place, just as it had been since Alison had died. The only joy that Jonathan seemed to have now was the port or the brandy, and the occasional visit from his father. Jonathan had even allowed his personal appearance to be neglected, and his entire demeanor caused those who were nearest to him some concern. Sir Robert decided that he should organize a "Spring Ball" and invitations were sent out to all his friends and acquaintances. Unsure if Jonathan would accept the invitation sent to him, Sir Robert personally visited the grieving young man, securing his promise to attend the ball. Jonathan, as suspected, was not really interested in attending any social gathering at this time, but he had given his word to Sir Robert and he could not fail his beloved Alison's father.

Sir Robert had taken the opportunity to invite some of his family and relations to the "Spring Ball," including Alison's cousin Barbara. There were those that Jonathan had met previously at his wedding, but there were others that he was yet to meet and this latter group included Barbara. Once again the society ladies attended in numbers to consider who among all the attending eligible bachelors would be suitable for their daughters. There was particular excitement when news spread that Jonathan Taylor was once again available and attending Sir Robert's ball. Barbara was among the first of Sir Robert's guests to be introduced to Jonathan, and she was immediately attracted to the brooding young man. She had come of age earlier in the year and she had been paraded to all the society gatherings by her parents, seeking a good match for her. Barbara, however, was very headstrong and knew her own mind. None of the young men to whom she had been introduced to thus far interested her more than the young, handsome, widower who was yet mourning for the loss of his young wife.

Barbara was a beautiful brunette with dark, smoldering eyes and a smile that could melt the coldest of hearts. There was a healthy hint of Rose in her skin and her features were so delicate one would be afraid to handle her in case she would break in your arms. Her voice was gentle and melodious, reminding him so much of his own dear wife who had passed away. Jonathan felt comfortable in her presence and, for the first time in many months, his heart felt so much lighter. All that evening he had watched as she danced with all the other young men of the county, and he felt pangs of jealousy as she smiled so alluringly in their company. He had, surprisingly, danced with Barbara himself and with his arms around her he felt as if he was waltzing on clouds. At the end of the evening he felt so happy, but it was coated by a deep sense of guilt that he had enjoyed himself so much, so soon after Alison's death.

To some people Barbara appeared to be a delicate, genteel, lady. But, in reality, Barbara, like her cousin Alison, enjoyed life to the full. She loved attending parties, singing the popular songs of the day, playing the piano, horse-riding, laughter and dancing. Jonathan pleased the young woman very much and she quickly came to understand just how her cousin Alison could have fallen so much in love with this man. Barbara could sense that she was losing her heart to this young man also, and she became determined that she would win him over to her. She could see that Jonathan was not interested in any of the other single ladies who had been brought to the ball by their parents to be paraded before him like so many prized animals.

As for Jonathan, he was still very confused about what his emotions were telling him. He felt guilty at the pleasure he had enjoyed in the company of another woman, but she had reminded him so much of his late, beloved, wife. He had gained a craving to be wrapped in the comforting arms of this new woman in his life, and to feel the beauty of her skin close to his. But, this was what troubled him so much, because he saw such thoughts as a betrayal of the love that he and Alison had for each other. Sir Robert could see the confusion in the mind of his son-in-law and decided to talk to him in a wise, fatherly manner. He began to open Jonathan's mind to the real possibility that Alison would have no wish to deprive her young husband of the love he needed. "It is time to move on," Sir Robert urged Jonathan while suggesting that Barbara would be the ideal choice for a new wife.

It was almost as if Jonathan had been given Alison's permission to get on with his life and like a helpless puppy he ran into Barbara's arms. She knew exactly what he craved and gave him everything he needed in bountiful supply. They went walking together and riding across the countryside together, talking about all sorts of things. Jonathan's grief was turned into happiness and the empty void that he had once in his heart was filled to overflowing by the love he began to feel for Barbara. That first kiss they shared sent a shiver of excitement down Jonathan's spine and, as their lips touched, he never wanted them to be parted again. So it continued for the next twelve months, in respect for the passing of his beloved Alison. But, within a month of the first anniversary of Alison's death the small Church at Ardcraig was filled to capacity with witnesses to the marriage of Barbara and

Jonathan. It was a time of great rejoicing, and the brightness and joy of the new life was reflected in "The Abbey". The local villagers and tenant farmers welcomed the new found happiness that their young master had discovered.

Barbara was as beautiful as Alison had once been. She was soft spoken and full of life, as Alison had once been. Just as Alison was deeply in love with her new husband, so Barbara loved every breath that Jonathan took. But, Barbara was very jealous of the strong hold that Alison's memory still had upon Jonathan's heart. She didn't mind him treasuring the memory of her dead cousin, but she wanted all of his love to be for her alone. Barbara had felt almost as if she had been sharing her new husband with his first wife and she now wanted this to stop. There was, as far as she was concerned, only one way to achieve her goal and that was to provide Jonathan with something Alison could not. Within a very few weeks of the wedding she came to Jonathan and announced that she was with child.

Jonathan was overjoyed with the news that he was to be a father, but his happiness was tempered by the great concerns he had about what had happened to his first wife. He need not have worried for Barbara bloomed in her pregnancy, at the end of which she produced a fine healthy boy who would be destined to carry on the "Taylor" name. Barbara, however, was not satisfied and wanted her son to have a companion in his childhood. As the third year of the marriage began Jonathan was presented with another son. Finally, in the fifth year of their marriage, Barbara announced excitedly that she was expecting yet another child. Jonathan felt so blessed that now, in his life, he had every thing a man in his position could want and he gave thanks for that.

Outside the great Irish Oak door that led into "The Abbey" stood an old, large, willow tree. Tradition spoke of the tree being magical in its power to reflect the fortunes of the "Taylor Family". It was said locally that this willow tree would fade and die only when the "Taylor Family" itself came to the end of its line and die. The truth of the legend was said to have been demonstrated in the year of Alison's death, when some branches died and the tree was greatly thinned out. The marriage to Barbara and the birth of Jonathan's first son brought a new lease of life to the willow tree. The green leaves of the willow swept down from the branches like so many individual waterfalls of lemon, green and gold. It was under this natural parasol Jonathan would sit, contemplate and thank God for all the blessings he had bestowed upon the family. He felt that in the strength and fertility of this willow that his family were destined to continue to prosper.

Meanwhile, in the village of Ardcraig, many of the people had almost forgotten the joy and the good times that existed in that year that Alison was "Lady of the Manor." She had been mistress for only twelve months, but in that time, she had made "The Abbey" beauty and light. The new mistress, Barbara, at first continued to treat the servants with gentleness and politeness, thus winning over their hearts. In Ardcraig itself she became a leading light in society, becoming known and respected because of her good, charitable works among the less fortunate. Jonathan, Barbara, and their children became known as "The Family in the Big House," and as they prospered so did all the people of the Ardcraig district. Barbara, as she had been with Jonathan, was envious of Alison's influence over the locals and she worked hard, in so many different ways, to ensure that that any residual memories would be wiped out.

In those first long and lonely months after Alison's death Jonathan wept great, bitter tears of grief for the loss of his great love. Servants despaired to see the young master standing alone over the grave of his wife, with a glass of wine in his hand and sobbing quietly. Angrily, he would call on God and ask him why his beautiful young wife was taken from this world, while their unborn child was not given the chance to know the love of its parents. He recalled the love, joy and excitement in Alison's beautiful eyes when she came to him with the news that she was expecting their child. At the same time he recalled the speed with which the brightness in the world suddenly disappeared when she was buried with their unborn child in that white coffin, so long ago.

The light in Jonathan's life did not return until Barbara arrived in his life. The numbness that had filled his body was gone and the despair, that had made his world so grey, was dispersed by her presence. With his new wife and children at his side Jonathan had renewed vigour and a determination to increase the size of his property. Unfortunately, he devoted so much time to his new wife and family that his visits to Alison's grave had decreased to a point where he never ventured there at all. Those wreaths and flowers, that Jonathan had once placed lovingly upon Alison's grave,were now rotting and being washed into the dark, insatiable ground just as her once beautiful body was six feet below the ground.

Despite the fact that the young couple had waited over a year after Alison's death, there were many of the older women of the village who felt uneasy about the speed in which Jonathan and Barbara had married. The servants at "The Abbey" eagerly gossiped about how he had neglected Alison's grave. There were rumours that all the little things that Alison had changed in the house had now been removed by Barbara, with Jonathan's agreement. They had seen how Jonathan's life had changed since he had married Barbara, but they did not like the way in which Alison's memory had been treated by the man for whom she had given her life. Some servants began to whisper quietly that Alison's spirit was unsettled by the turn of events in her husband's life. They talked about how she would make her spirit visible, and that she had been seen wandering "The Abbey" at night, by 'reliable sources'. The 'reliable sources' described the apparition as gliding along in a white shroud and in her pale, shadowy arms she held the body of a child close to her.

As the years passed the reports of Alison's spirit appearing became more frequent among the residents of Ardcraig, and many began avoiding the grounds of "The Abbey" at night. At the same time the servants decided it was best to not tell Jonathan anything about Alison's spirit appearing. From the beginning of her marriage Barbara kept a close watch over her new husband and home. She overshadowed those who visited him, and she quickly began removing any item that might even remind him of Alison. As Barbara concentrated on removing every trace of her cousin's memory she became more and more obsessed with Alison's life in "The Abbey". One of the first things Barbara removed from the house was the cradle, which Alison had prepared for the birth of her child. It had, of course, never been occupied but, nonetheless, Barbara decided that it would go. To soften the blow for Jonathan she convinced him that it should be given to one of the less fortunate families in Ardcraig as part of her wider charitable program. This program was financed through the removal and sale or donation of Alison's trinkets. All the baby's clothes that Alison had collected and personally sewn were given away, as were a great number of her dresses and coats. Barbara wanted rid of every item and to ensure that the wardrobes and cupboards were filled only with those things that belonged to her.

They say that " a new broom always sweeps clean", and Barbara scoured the house, room by room, for any item that may once have belonged to Alison. Whatever she did not give away, she burned and Jonathan was left completely unaware of what was happening. The only time he was consulted was when Barbara began to change the décor of the house, the paintings and portraits, curtains and furnishings. In a very short period of time Barbara's plan was complete and even the memory of Alison's beautiful face had disappeared.

Barbara, just as she had intended, was the center of her husband's life and he, for his part, was ecstatically happy with his passionate young wife, and the wonderful children she had bore him. The sorrow he had suffered so deeply in his heart had been replaced by a life that was now filled with tenderness and love.

It had taken Barbara a considerably longer period of time to win over the hearts of those servants and villagers who held very fond memories of Jonathan's first wife. Gradually, one by one, many of these people fell under Barbara's spell. Only those who declared that they had witnessed Alison's white, shrouded apparition, gliding around "The Abbey" and its grounds held fast. Inside the house Alison's pet dog resisted all of Barbara's efforts to befriend her. "Sam" was a small, shaggy "Yorkshire Terrier", who had grown old and weary since his mistress had departed this life. Alison had raised "Sam" from a puppy, pampering him, playing with him, and teasing him with all sorts of playthings and treats to eat. When Alison died, however, "Sam" fretted terribly, growing old and weary almost overnight. During her funeral and for many weeks afterward, the dog whimpered almost incessantly as it wandered from room to room in an almost ceaseless search for his young mistress. After a period of time the dog stopped its search and satisfied itself by following Jonathan on each and every occasion that he visited Alison's graveside. Even after Jonathan had stopped his visits to the grave, "Sam" would go there alone and lie there atop of Alison's grave for hour after hour as if protecting her from harm.

Because of "Sam's" attitude toward her Barbara could not tolerate its presence in the house. She also resented the way that the dog always wandered to the forgotten graveside and, in an effort to bring this canine pilgrimage to an end she told the servants to permanently close the gate to the grave. Although she had now barred the dog's means of reaching his former mistress' resting place, "Sam" would walk daily to the locked gate where he would lie down to show that he, at least, had not forgotten Alison. All Barbara's efforts to turn the dog's affections had failed. In her determination to remove any trace of Alison Barbara now turned her attention to "Sam", who had consistently snapped and growled at her. Barbara had tried every possible way to make herself acceptable to "Sam" but all her soft overtures were received with snarls and the uncovering of strong, dangerous, white teeth. In the beginning she was sympathetic to "Sam's" misery, his restlessness, his whining and she was saddened by the channels that its tears had worn under those faithful eyes. She had tried to take the dog into her arms to comfort him, but "Sam" had snapped at her in his efforts to escape. Jonathan moved against the dog but Barbara, at that time, insisted everything was alright, though she made no more efforts to comfort the dog.

After this incident "Sam" was removed from its resting place in the warm living-room. Never again did that dog stretch itself on the rug before the blazing log-fire that would be lit in the hearth. That day of "Sam's" exile was a particularly cold and stormy autumnal day. The gale-force winds had caused many shipwrecks, and there was much mourning in the villages for drowned husbands and sons, whose small fishing boats had been sucked into the boiling surges. The roar of the wind caused a tumult in the air, assisted by the creaking and lashing of the trees blowing in wild confusion. The rain pelted down upon the ground causing puddles to form and soil to be washed away.

In "The Abbey" there were attics and gable-end rooms that had little light and were seldom visited. Entry to these rooms from the inhabited areas of the house was by a corkscrew staircase, narrow and steep. None of the servants enjoyed the prospect of visiting these uppermost rooms. Among themselves the servants talked about hearing creaking footsteps on the floors at night, or the occasional slamming of a door, or the squeak of a rusty hinge on a window that was stealthily opening. Some servants who had braved the attic rooms complained that locked doors suddenly opened, and previously bolted windows were found unbolted. As the wind blew through every crevice in that old building its wailed like a banshee. Then, one bright snowy morning, a housemaid was obliged to go to the attic where she discovered a small, wet, footprint on the floor. It looked as if this footprint was from someone who had come barefoot through the snow. The housemaid let out a scream and fled back down the steep, narrow, staircase.

In one of the attics, tucked away in a corner, stood a great hasped chest, inside of which some of Alison's clothes lay mouldering. This wooden chest was locked, and was likely to remain so, for Barbara had taken the key and disposed of it. From the high, but small, attic windows there was a glorious view of the land. The viewer could see the red sandstone valleys where deer could be found feeding. In the distance was the dark wood, whose trees tossed in the breeze and, nearer hand, the herd of cattle, grazing quietly on the master's land. But viewers were few and far between and not one of the servants would go near those windows without expecting to be touched by some icy-cold finger on the shoulder. Any whose business brought them to the attic always glanced toward the dark nervously anticipating something would happen. Though few went there alone they talked about strange earthy smells and a bitter chill, even on the warmest days. The man whom Jonathan employed as gamekeeper told the story that one night he had seen a faint moving glow from an attic window, followed by a wavering shadow.

In that cold attic, where the chest stood, "Sam" took up his new residence. One morning the dog had followed a servant up to that room and when he saw the chest he began to whimper excitedly. "Sam" sniffed and rubbed himself against the chest and, finally lay on top of the old chest with his nose resting on his paws. From that moment the small dog refused to leave its new residence. Finally, the servants stopped their efforts to coax "Sam" back into the real world and, out of pity for him, spread a warm rug for him over the chest. Jonathan no longer asked about the whereabouts of the dog, and Barbara was simply not interested where it was. The servants, however, saw the dog every day and fed it with food scraps. As time passed "Sam" grew older and almost blind. The house servants never neglected him and he would allow them to pet him and play with him at their leisure.

Those who witnessed the events said that when the hall clock struck midnight the small dog could be heard scampering down from the attic. None understood how the dog could come out of a room that had its door locked. Nevertheless, the dog trotted alongside a barely visible form. The witnesses said they could hear a faint rustle as if a silk gown was trailing from step to step, and sometimes "Sam" would bark sharply like any playful puppy, leaping up to lick some unseen hand. Most of the servants, however, would close the doors to their rooms when the first chimes of midnight struck from the hall clock. They could still hear the patter of "Sam's" tiny paws and his excited bark. Though filled with awe that the spirit of the dead might be present, they were assured that the spirit would not harm them. These same servants may pay homage to the new mistress, but they fondly recalled the gentleness and purity of the first wife.

Wondering what had caused Alison's spirit to return, many suggested that she may have come back for the sake of another. Jonathan and Barbara were always in their own bedroom when the spirit passed. The spirit went everywhere through the house checking that windows and doors were fastened securely, as she had done when she was mistress. Those were the days when her young husband would lovingly declare that the house was only precious because it held her. The servants now considered this spirit of the former mistress to be a guardian against evil. One night a candle had been carelessly left alight, and the nearest curtain to the flame caught fire. In the silence of the night the flames were extinguished by someone, or something, unknown. In the morning the house awakened to a charred curtain, but no sign of what had caused the accidental fire to be extinguished.

Barbara, of course, had heard the stories of the spirit wandering the house and grounds, but insisted these should be kept from Jonathan. She always ensured that they would avoid contact with any spirit by being in their bed before midnight chimed. Then, one night, as Jonathan lay in bed finishing some book-work, he asked Barbara if she would retrieve a notebook from the desk in his office. She was sitting at her dressing table combing her long, black, hair and turned to look at her husband with some disdain. It was near midnight and she was not prepared to be accompanied by the spirit of her dead cousin. She moved to the bedroom door, fixing her hair as best she could, but as she put her hand to the handle of the door she told him, "No!"

"Pardon?" Jonathan questioned with some surprise.

"I will not go downstairs," Barbara told him. "I will not go anywhere until that devil of a dog and his companion pass by and return to their lair."

Jonathan laughed quietly at the unexpected fear that his wife was showing. Barbara angrily opened the bedroom door and stared into the darkness of the unlit landing. Then, descending the stairs, Barbara heard the patter of tiny dog paws on the polished wood. Jonathan also heard the sound of the dog's paws, but he could also hear another sound. It was the swishing sound of a silken gown keeping pace with the descent of the dog. "What is that?" he asked.

Barbara slammed the bedroom door closed and told him, "It is the spirit of your first wife. She has haunted this place for years, and everyone knows but you!"'

"Alison?"

"Yes, Alison. She has not forgotten us as much as we have forgotten her."

The haunting continued for several years after this incident and Jonathan was easily persuaded to move into the house that had been left to him by Alison's father. "The Abbey" was abandoned along with its canine resident. Several years later "Sam's" body was found lying across Alison's neglected grave. From that moment no encounters with the spirit of Alison were reported, but Jonathan would not return to his former home. People in the area still insist that there is a presence about the house, even though it is virtually a ruin after so many decades of neglect

REMEMBERING MINNIE

The years had not been good to "Wee Minnie". Now an elderly lady of over eighty years she had lived in this same village for all her life and, not surprisingly, was well known in the area. She was born the long awaited and only child of a small farmer and his wife, whose property lay to the southern edge of the village. Whenever Minnie had cause to recall her childhood on that farm she always did so with great affection, and shed a tear to the memory of beloved parents who showered their love upon her. After her parents passed on Minnie inherited the small farm and in which she was born, and in which she had spent so many years. Several months later there was a knock on the front door of the cottage, which she opened to find the caller was a young man called Sean O'Donnell.

Sean O'Donnell was not a complete stranger to Minnie. In fact, as an agricultural laborer, Sean had worked many times for Minnie's father and he now called to see how he could help Minnie on the farm. He had been at the wake of both parents, the father being the most recent, and there Sean had promised to assist Minnie when it was time to plough and plant. However, working in such close proximity brought the two young people together romantically. Sean was a fine young man, only five years older than Minnie and very highly respected among the farming community in the district. Minnie fell head over heels in love with the young man, while he became completely entrapped by the beauty of the young woman. Eventually Sean gathered the courage to ask her to marry him and, overjoyed by his proposal, Minnie eagerly accepted.

Minnie had been a beautiful bride on that fine, late Spring day and all who saw the young couple on their wedding day remarked on how well they were matched. Sean and Minnie were indeed well matched, but neither of these two young people had much of a financial status. The small farm that Minnie had inherited was not now financially viable. Events had moved on since her father's day on the land and, despite Sean's best efforts, Minnie decided it was best to sell her small piece of land and cottage. Some of the money she received from the sales she used to pay for her wedding to Sean. To his credit, Sean O'Donnell was much respected in the district as a hard, conscientious worker, and he was seldom without work of one kind or another. There were numerous large farms in the area that relied heavily on agricultural laborers to work the land. Sean, when he took Minnie as his wife, chose to give up the life of a jobbing laborer, choosing to take a permanent position on a large farm that provided the young couple with a "tied cottage." Fortunately for Minnie the cottage was in the nearby village of "Cnochmedown" where the couple would spend all of their married life. In that small cottage Minnie gave birth to their first and only child, a boy to whom they gave the name Peter. After years of hard, honest toil Sean came to the point in his life when he had to retire from work. It was a point which Sean had never wanted to reach, but his hard work and loyalty were well rewarded. As a retirement present Sean's grateful employer gifted the cottage to him and Minnie for the remainder of their days.

Sean and Minnie lived many long and happy years together in that small cottage until, at the age of seventy-three years, Sean was diagnosed with a particularly aggressive form of cancer. In the beginning of the illness Sean had only suffered some slight discomfort, but his condition deteriorated very quickly and he had to undergo a period of chemo-therapy treatment. Although this treatment had considerable positive affects on many others, in Sean's case it was unsuccessful. Over the previous month if anything, the chemo-therapy given to Sean only appeared to aggravate the poor man's condition. Over the last month of his life Sean suffered great pain until, finally, he mercifully passed away just before his seventy-fifth birthday. It was a credit to his reputation and the high regard with which he was held among his neighbors that his funeral was so well attended. Almost the entire population of the village and surrounding district turned out to witness the burial of Sean O'Donnell. For several months afterward Minnie had no real concerns as she had her grown-up son for support and her neighbors all rallied around her.

When Sean had died, not surprisingly, Minnie looked to her unmarried son, Peter, to help her face the harsh realities of the world without her husband's strong, guiding hand. She relied on Peter to step easily into his father 's shoes and proved himself to be a good provider for them both. The young man, however, had been spoiled all his life and a sense of responsibility was something he had not cultivated. There were those in the village who agreed that Peter had no sense of what real work was. He believed, rather, that he was so special that the world owed him a living, assured that others should and would look after him. Since the day he left school, shortly after his fourteenth birthday, Peter had worked at numerous jobs, but he could not hold on to any of these positions for more than two years. He had no work ethic and lacked any sense of accountability, always taking the easy way rather than the right way to do a job. Whenever an employer decided that he'd had enough of his slap-dash methods Peter would be dismissed. On these regular occasions Peter would go to his parents and assure them that the loss of the job was never his fault.

Minnie was a doting mother and always had a sympathetic ear for any excuse her son would give. Sean, as a loving father, would always do whatever he could to obtain a new position for his son. He, of course, was fully aware of his son's failings but he kept his patience with Peter for the sake of the love he had for Minnie. On many occasions Sean had tried to work with his ne'er do well son, but his efforts were always frustrated by Peter's attitude. The young man, unlike his father, gained for himself a reputation for being idle, argumentative, unreliable and for being too fond of his ale and spirits. It was well known that most of the money Peter earned, or 'borrowed' from his parents, usually found its way into Dinny McKeevers pocket through the cash register at the local public house. Inside Dinny's pub Peter would often drink until he could hardly stand straight and his pockets were empty. There he would amply demonstrate his talent for bad language, bad manners, and the bad-mouthing of his employers, all of which served only to ensure many turned against him. In fact, Peter's only 'friends' came from among those local men who were every bit as shiftless and idle as he was.

When Sean O'Donnell gave up his last breath all those people who had held him in high regard believed that, now he was gone, they no longer had to bear Peter's attitudes. In time past they had given Peter jobs because of the respect that they had for Sean and Minnie. Sean's death had relieved them of any need to suffer Peter's presence any longer, though they still retained a deep respect for Minnie. She, however, was devastated by the death of Sean and she grieved bitterly for the loss of such a loyal and loving husband. Sean had never seen his family in need of anything in this world, but things would definitely change now that he was gone. When Minnie had cause to turn to her son for emotional and financial support, at this difficult time in her life, she found Peter wanting in both areas.

Peter was the sort of person who blamed everyone but himself for his misfortunes. When his father died he failed to take any positive role and support his elderly mother. He preferred to stay at home, groaning about the fact that he could not find work in the area, though others could. When Minnie pressed him on this Peter would tell her that the neighbors had all turned against him, and that they were conspiring to ensure that he would never be able to earn an honest living for himself. He never once suggested that making an honest living for himself was, actually, the last thing on his mind. Finally, about a month after Sean's funeral, Peter came to his mother and told her that he was leaving the village. His intention, he said, was to move to England where he could find well-paid work and live a better style of life. "My only difficulty," he told Minnie, "is that I have no money to get to England."

He knew that with his father gone his mother only had a small income, mostly pension money. This, of course, made little difference to Peter and he began playing on the emotional sensitivities of his elderly mother. Callously Peter demanded that he be given his share of whatever his father had left to them both. Minnie could not bear to admit to her son that his father had seen fit to leave him nothing in his will. Sean, in his wisdom, believed that he and Minnie had already funded Peter's life more than sufficiently and he left him nothing. Minnie had been left whatever small amount of money that they had gathered, in the knowledge that she would ensure it was not wasted. However, in her grief, Minnie gave in to the demands of her beloved son and she promised to give him three thousand pounds. It was every last penny she and Sean had saved over the years in the local branch of the "Credit Union". This represented all that she had of value in the world.

Peter didn't know that this represented everything his mother had. Even if he had known, it is doubtful if it would have made any difference to him. He pressed Minnie continuously until she finally gave in and went to get it. Peter knew exactly what he was going to do with the money and he was impatient to have it in his hands. Once Minnie handed him the cash Peter packed a case for himself, kissed his mother goodbye, and wasted no time in scuttling out of the village on the first available bus. As he kissed his mother farewell, Peter held her close to him and promised her that he would write to her regularly, sending money home to her whenever he could. The first letter that Minnie received arrived three weeks after Peter had left the village. She was, of course, overjoyed to receive a letter from her son in England and she proudly told ever person she met that her son was living in Birmingham working in a car factory. Minnie was thrilled to hear that he had managed to get himself a well-paid job that allowed him to have his own flat and a car. Peter had closed his letter sending all his love and he promised that he would write again soon, enclosing a few pounds.

That one and only letter from Peter had arrived five years ago and, since that time, nothing further. She had taken note of the address that Peter had put on his letter and she had written to him every week for the first year of his absence. Minnie had never received a reply to any of those many letters she had sent and she even planned to go to Birmingham herself to seek him out. Unfortunately Minnie was never able to gather enough money that would buy her a ticket, or pay for her stay there. She only wanted to see his face once again and discover if he was safe. Every day for those five long years Minnie had prayed Peter would write and she waited hopefully every morning for the tell-tale sign that she had received a letter. Those lonely days had turned into weeks, and those weeks turned into months. All the while

Minnie received no letters, no postcards, no birthday or Christmas cards, and no postal orders.

Minnie found the loneliest and hardest time of the year, without her son, to be Christmas. For days and weeks before the event she could look out for her front window and see cards and parcels being delivered to every house in the village except for her's. It was a miserable time. Beside there being no letter from Peter, there was no other person with whom Minnie could fully share the festive joy. In Minnie's home a couple of slices of chicken breast, with some pre-packed mashed potato and a small tin of peas, usually took the place of a turkey dinner and all its usual festive trimmings. And yet, despite the sorrows of her lonely life, Minnie always attempted to put on a brave face in front of her neighbors. Every time she met one of her neighbors she would smile at them and bring them up to date on her son's life in England. Minnie was, of course, just keeping up appearances by telling them that Peter, "Sure he's living the great life over there." Unknown to Minnie the neighbors already knew the truth but said nothing.

The people of "Cnochmedun" knew Peter well and were fully aware of the sort of man that he was. It is not surprising, therefore, that they harbored doubts about Peter keeping regular contact and suddenly becoming industrious. They did, however, respect Minnie and for this reason they chose not to give her any sign that they doubted her reports of Peter's activity. There was one particular question that none of the neighbors ever asked because they already knew the answer. They would never ask Minnie if Peter was coming home for Christmas. Every person in the village were well aware that Minnie's son had never returned home one time since he left the village five years previously. Nevertheless, some close neighbors were concerned enough about Minnie's welfare that they kept an eye on her especially when the cold, winter, weather settled in.

Minnie was not the type of person to complain and she was a woman whose pride would not permit her to even consider accepting charity from anyone. Those who asked about her welfare were usually met with a kindly smile and a polite rebuff, "Sure I am doing great. I am snug and warm here."

Some would aske "Have you everything you need, Minnie?"

"More than enough," she would reply. "Peter often sends me a few pounds, which help a lot in this weather."

None of this was true and Minnie felt miserable having to be so deceitful to people who were her friends, and genuinely concerned about her. But Peter was still her son and Minnie would never willingly allow him to be seen in a bad light by others. Since he was a young boy Minnie had wanted him to be considered a loving and caring person. Sadly, Minnie's neighbors were very much aware of just what kind of person Peter O'Donnell actually was. Some neighbors were also aware of the predicament in which he had left his mother when he disappeared to England, leaving her alone. But, while they knew the truth about Peter they also knew how much he meant to Minnie and they would never upset that old woman, for whom they had much regard.

One of Minnie's most attentive neighbours was Dan Corkery and his wife, Sarah. Dan was the village postman and highly regarded as a man of discretion and integrity. In fact you would be hard put to find any person in the village who would have a bad word to say about Dan, or his wife. Every morning, irrespective of weather conditions, Dan would walk past by Minnie's front door with his heavy post-bag over his shoulder. He couldn't fail to notice the elderly lady looking hopefully out of the window for him to bring a letter to her door. There were days when there were letters to be delivered to Minnie's house, but these days were far outnumbered by the days when there were none. Nonetheless, whether he delivered letters or not, Dan would always wave at Minnie and give her one of his broadest, friendly smiles. Every morning Minnie would return Dan's wave and acknowledge him with a friendly smile of her own.

On those days when he had no letters to deliver to Minnie, Dan was well aware of the great disappointment she was feeling. Those days on which he had letters for her he could see the bright look of hope sweep across her face and knew that the light would be dimmed when Minnie saw the letters were not from Peter. Being the village postman, Dan was aware of postmarks and other things that confirmed letters were not from Peter. Moreover, Dan knew the truth about Peter O'Donnell and the wastrel he was. He was also aware that Peter never sent his mother even a postcard in all the time that he had been away in England.

On those rare occasions when Dan would push letters through her letter-box, she would wait patiently for a moment until she waved at Dan as he proceeded on with his 'round'. This done she would rush as fast as she could to her front door, eager to see if there was some communication from Peter. Minnie would bend down slowly and gather up the letters from the rug that covered the wooden hall-floor at the foot of the door. Once she had them in her hands, Minnie would shuffle through them quickly, inspecting the postmarks and writing. She always expected that she would come across at least one letter that her son had sent. On most occasions Minnie would shuffle the letters and inspect them more than once, unconvinced that once again Peter had failed to write. But, once she had been convinced, Minnie would slowly shuffle back to her favorite armchair in the living-room, where she would shed a quiet, private tear.

It was, undoubtedly, the loneliness that was proving to be her greatest burden in her life. In the winter months, especially, when days were short and the nights were long, she felt the loneliness even more. The cold, wet weather kept people off the streets and she had little to occupy her mind during those long hours of inactivity. There were the daily papers, the television and the radio, but none of these could replace the company and joy of another human presence. Once the paper was read from cover to cover it only left the radio and television for company, and their novelty soon wore thin.

Over the previous few years both Dan and his wife, Sarah, had taken it upon themselves to visit Minnie on a regular basis. Other than these the only other regular visitor was the Parish Priest, Father Donnelly, every first Friday of the month as part of his pastoral duties towards the sick and the elderly. Dan, of course, saw Minnie every morning while on his postal round in the village. But, on a Saturday, Dan would usually leave Minnie's house until last and he would always knock on her door. The old, lonely woman always looked forward to Dan calling on Saturday because she could invite him into the house for a cup of tea. Dan, being the man he was never refused. His wife, Sarah, would call with Minnie every Friday afternoon, after her shift at the local creamery had finished. Sarah had always been fond of Minnie and she looked on the visit as being more of a friendly call than a good deed. She would always collect what little grocery shopping that Minnie required, and she would always bring the old lady's newspaper money to pay the newsagent. For Minnie Sarah's visit was an opportunity to socialize with another female. It really was just a good, old gossip session over a cup of tea and some biscuits. At the same time it proved to be excellent therapy for an old, lonely woman. Sarah could keep her informed of all the new happenings in the village. Minnie enjoyed hearing about the engagements, marriages, births, and even the deaths that had occurred. But, most of all, Minnie enjoyed the more 'juicy' gossip that Sarah would bring and, whatever Sarah didn't know, Dan would always let Minnie know the rest. She had discovered that Sarah had quite the 'nose' for the more interesting gossip of the village. She could keep the old lady up to date on who was cheating on whom, or who had gotten themselves into trouble, and what husband or wife had deserted their spouse. Not surprisingly, then, Minnie really enjoyed her visits from Dan and Sarah but, sadly, they were too short.

Each day of Minnie's lonely life was virtually the same as the day before. She was used to rising early every morning, and she would prepare her meager breakfast of porridge, followed by tea, toast and marmalade. Dishes cleared and cleaned Minnie would sit in her comfortable armchair beside a fire that would remain unlit for most of the day. Even on the coldest, winter's day the fire would remain unlit until evening because the price of coal and turf made it too expensive for Minnie to have it lit all day. It was not because of any miserliness on her part. All she had was her pension and she had to manage this carefully if she was to heat her home and feed herself. It was hard on such a meager income to finance the necessities and there was nothing left for the purchase of luxuries.

Since the death of her husband Minnie's only income had been her pension. Any money that had been saved by her and her husband had been given to their son, Peter, to finance a new start in England. She may have been due more in State Benefits, but Minnie was too proud to be thought of as a beggar to pursue her entitlements. When it was cold she put on an extra coat, or jumper, or blanket to keep warm. The television, as in most homes, took pride of place in the living-room. But Minnie's television was an old model, long past its replacement date, and it was only switched on for a few hours in the evening because Minnie was concerned about the charge on the electric bill. For this reason most of Minnie's entertainment came from a small, battery-powered radio that she had persuaded Dan to set on a local radio station's wavelength. As far as diet was concerned it was also simple and sparse. Porridge, tea and toast, baked beans, eggs and ham were her main dietary staples. A roast dinner of any kind was a luxury rather than a regular part of her diet. Despite the fact that Minnie suffered because her body lacked certain dietary vitamins. This restricted lifestyle had been forced upon her by the financial situation caused by the actions of her son. All Minnie could do was to keep a happy face despite the hardships, and continue to smile so that the tears could not fall.

We have spoken on several occasions about how difficult a time Christmas was for Minnie, both financially and emotionally. Sitting in her lonely armchair, wrapped in a fleece blanket for extra warmth, Minnie would stare at the world outside through her living-room window.Up and down the village, people were busily making their preparations for the Christmas season. In the center of the village a Christmas tree had been raised outside the main gate of the Church, and dressed with what seemed to be hundreds of blue and red LED lights. Between the lamp-posts that stood on each side of the village's main through road were strung Multi-colored lights of red, blue, white, yellow and green. The night the lights were switched on Minnie watched from her living-room window. A local dignitary made a short speech before he pulled the switch, and the children from the local school led the gathered residents in singing a variety of well known Christmas carols. Then, every morning, as the great day approached Minnie watched Dan scurry from door to door weighed down with parcels and Christmas cards. Villagers would process up and down the village's main road carrying fresh Christmas trees, Christmas decorations and Christmas presents. Inside Minnie's house, however, the decorations and preparations were different and fewer in number.

A few strands of silver, gold, red and green tinsel were strung over the branches of an old and dusty man-made Christmas tree. There were none of the multi-colored fairy-lights that you would expect to see adorning the tree. There were no traditional holly and ivy to decorate the fireplace or picture frames, and no mistletoe to catch the unwary. Although it was the season for everyone to feel jolly and share all the good things in life, there was not much in Minnie's life for her to feel jolly about. Nevertheless, Minnie always tried her best to show a happy face to all who met her. At Christmas she could look back on those days when she, Sean and Peter shared so much yuletide joy. Nowadays Minnie's only Christmas cheer came when Dan and Sarah would call to visit.

Every Christmas Eve, after making his last delivery, Dan would collect his wife and they would call at Minnie's house. There they would exchange small Christmas gifts, have some tea and Christmas loaf, and toast the birth of Christ with a hot whisky or two. When it came to Christmas presents, Minnie never received many and, because of her financial straits, she could not afford to give many. The local "St. Vincent de Paul" group would always deliver a small hamper of Christmas food, or a bag of coal, to all the elderly and the needy of the Parish. Her only other gift would be a tin of "Fox's Assorted Biscuits" from Dan and Sarah, both of whom were well aware of Minnie's sweet-tooth. Minnie, in return, would wrap a small box of chocolates or other sweets, which she would present to a very appreciative Dan and Sarah. They were both well aware that Minnie could not afford much in the way of presents but, at the same time, they wouldn't dream of hurting the old woman by suggesting it was not necessary for her to buy them something.

Minnie had, for many years, longed to have been able to send some kind of present to Peter for Christmas. But the old woman had not received any news about her son in five years and did not know where she would send one. Even if she could afford a present to send she could not quite think of what Peter would like. Maybe it was more than just apathy that made her feel this way. Christmas in Minnie's life was gradually becoming irrelevant and the years of loneliness were beginning to tell on her health. Over the previous twelve months her rheumatic arthritis had worsened, causing her to shuffle along rather than walk steadily, lifting her feet one in front of the other. The Doctor, another rare visitor to Minnie's home, had diagnosed her as suffering from "Unstable Angina" and had prescribed appropriate medication for her condition. But Minnie continued to feel breathless and tired almost all the time, a condition that did little to ease her increasingly depressed state of mind. All of these things combined to confine Minnie to a cold, unheated house, each and every day. What made it worse was the realization that there was little prospect of a change for the better. Privately, Minnie began to feel so low in spirits that she secretly began to pray that this Christmas may be her last, leaving her to peacefully join her much missed husband in the local graveyard. She kept such thoughts to herself, but both Dan and Sarah were now aware that her spirit had decreased and they knew what had caused this.

Christmas Eve had arrived with a hard, heavy blast of ice-cold air that quickly covered the entire district with a light coating of white frost that crunched under foot. Early in the morning several members from the "St. Vincent de Paul Society" called at Minnie's, bringing a hamper and a large bag of coal with them. It was a bright spot on an otherwise bitterly cold morning because, for the first in a long while, Minnie could light her fire and let it burn all day. This was a luxury that Minnie would enjoy, sitting in her comfortable armchair with a cup of warm tea in her hand. No blanket or extra coat was needed that morning for every bit of warmth that she needed was being radiated from the glowing red, coals in the hearth.

The deep darkness of a mid-winter evening had descended over the village when a very recognizable knock on the front door was heard. Slowly and carefully Minnie raised herself out of her armchair and shuffled toward the front-door. As she opened the door she saw

Dan Corkery standing there and he greeted her warmly with, "Merry Christmas, Minnie."

"Merry Christmas, Dan," Minnie replied, returning the postman's cheery smile. "Come on in and warm yourself by the fire," she invited him.

Without a second thought Dan accepted the invitation and stepped into the cottage. Closing the front door behind him, Dan followed Minnie into the living-room. He announced, "I 've brought a wee bit of the good stuff." Lifting his right hand he showed Minnie the half-bottle of "Bushmill's Whisky" that he had brought with him.

"Our wee Christmas treat," laughed Minnie.

"For medicinal purposes only, of course," teased Dan.

"Oh, Of course!" Minnie laughed. "Purely medicinal."

Minnie sat down again on her armchair and told Dan, "The medicine glasses are in the sideboard."

Dan poured the smooth tasting, golden liquid into two glasses he had retrieved from the sideboard. "Just a wee drop of the pure stuff first," he told Minnie as he handed her one of the glasses. "Before we dilute it with hot water, sugar and lemon," he smiled.

Then, lifting their glasses the two friends toasted each other, "Merry Christmas and a Happy New Year."

The two friends sat together in the living-room drinking their whiskies and gossiping about the latest events in the village. As usual there were a few surprises and a few laughs at the antics of some village folk. But, as he came near to the end of his drink, Dan excused himself and went into the kitchen to put the kettle on to boil. "The kettle will soon be boiled and we will have a couple of hot one's," he told Minnie as he made his way back into the living-room. There was new knock on the front door and Dan moved to answer it. "Sit where you are," he told Minnie. "I'll get the door."

Dan moved into the hall and opened the door to find Sarah standing on the step. "It's only Sarah and a friend," he explained.

"Bring them in for a wee drink," she insisted.

Dan led the way into the living-room with Sarah following close behind him, obscuring the guest from Minnie's view for a moment. As they came further into the room Minnie recognized the features of her son, Peter, and could not quite quite believe what she was seeing. Putting her hands to her mouth she rose up from her chair and let out a squeal of utter joy as tears filled her eyes. Peter came closer to her and she threw her arms around his neck, holding her close to him.

"I am so sorry, Mother", he wept as he embraced her.

"Be quiet now, son," she said soothingly as the tears flowed down her cheeks. "You are home now and safe again."

Dan and Sarah turned to each other and smiled. Sarah wiped a tear from her eyes, took Dan's hand in hers and, together, they left the house to Minnie and her prodigal son.

TWO WEE ONES

Poteen

We Irishmen have always held that we are nothing less than the best connoisseurs of the finest whisky. Moreover, we will argue that Ireland is the true home of whisky and the best of the world's whiskies originate in this small island. Paying due respect to our Scottish cousins we will only submit that Scotch Whiskey comes a distant second in terms of taste and quality. Our pride in our product is such that we use only the highest quality ingredients to ensure that the quality of our whisky is unsurpassed. But not satisfied with this alone, Irish Whisky is triple distilled to ensure a smoothness that other whiskies cannot attain.

It is in the nature of human beings to doubt the assurances given to them by others. In this case, if you have doubts about the assurances you are given, then I suggest you test Irish Whisky for yourself. The cultured whisky drinker will certainly agree that Scotch and other attempts to produce a top grade, classic whisky are not as smooth as "Irish" on the throat and taste buds. However, even I will submit to the argument that "Irish Poteen", properly made, is superior to "Irish Whisky." The only problem with the Poteen is the fact that it is illegal to produce this favorite Irish beverage. Of course some business entrepreneurs have now began producing "legal poteen", but do not be fooled because it is only a poor copy of the real thing.

Let us consider the real thing and its benefits to the human being. As you no doubt know, no true Irishman will allow something as trivial as illegality to prevent him from enjoying the best this world has to offer. "O, divine poteen," it has been hailed and others have called it, "The Nectar of the Gods." But, irrespective of what people call it, they will all agree that in its clear liquid form the poteen is nothing less than the immortal essence of barley, grown in the fertile fields of Ireland, and left to ripen in the sun. No Irishman would consider putting any other drink, liquor or wine on a par with poteen, knowing that to do so is sacrilege, and a betrayal of his traditions.

Just as distillers of Irish Whisky triple distill their product for smoothness, so too the poteen makers triple distill their much sought after refreshment. There the similarity ends. We know that by triple distilling the liquid makes it smoother, but it also concentrates the alcohol content. While Irish whiskey, God bless it, is triple distilled the manufacturers are under a legal obligation to dilute the whisky with water. They also store it in oak casks that have previously been used to store Sherry and from these casks it takes on flavour and colouring. Unfortunately people have started to add water, lemonade, coke and soda water to their whisky. When an Irishman drinks whisky he drinks only Irish whiskey. But when he drinks water, lemonade, coke, or soda water with his whisky then you will know he is an impostor.

Whisky in the Gaelic language is called "Uisce Beatha" or "Water of Life," and was a derivative of poteen. In bygone centuries the Gods of Ireland, "The Tuatha de Danaan" began the distillation process and gave it to the people of Ireland. From this time the poteen was considered to be a divine gift. Furthermore, as well as being a refreshing drink it was said to have almost magical powers to cure all male and female problems. For those with high blood pressure, or suffer from anxiety, poteen acts as a relaxant and one glass per day can bring a soothingness to a person and gradually restore their equilibrium. In cases where the blood is heated the poteen can help cool the blood, in both men and women, making them more congenial and bestows a spirit of love and friendship that can open the heart to romance. Furthermore, a glass of poteen can bring about a gentle chastening and change in one's soul. It has been known to have very positive affects on a person's sense of generosity, kindness, and even their courage. Very importantly the poteen helps to remove those negative things that trouble both men and women by causing them to set aside their cares and, thereby, avoid potential calamities.

You might say that there is no proof that poteen can provide men and women with such benefits. In response I would simply ask you to consider those men and women who have given good cause for Ireland to be called *"The Land of Saints and Scholars"*. It could be pointed out that "Saints", however, have no need for poteen since they have God and prayer to see them through their difficulties. But, is it not sinful if God gives us something that is beneficial to us and we fail to help ourselves to it. Just as in today's world alcohol has many uses medicinally, so it was in those days of St. Patrick, St. Kevin, St. Columba, and St. Bridgid. And what about the "Scholars", for which Ireland is famed for producing and still turns out? We all know that the artistic temperament is very finely balanced instrument that is given to few in this world. Fame and fortune are magnificent things to have, of course, but they can also be deadly parasites that can eat away at our confidence and general mental health. Once a person attains fame it acts like a drug, of which they must have more and more. Without this drug they despair and fall into ruination. Many of the men and women artists, poets, authors, engineers and inventors have taken the poteen to help them keep their 'balance'. Some have used it to help change them into a more assured person, creating new treasures for us to enjoy.

It is at this point that I must now, sadly, issue a word of caution by admitting that poteen, powerful as it is, is not for every person. Before others say it I will admit that there are in our world some very unfortunate people for whom alcohol is devastating. Those people should pay heed to my warning and stay away from the poteen. Such people can have a great susceptibility to the ordinary, run-of-the-mill, alcoholic beverages, which are not as pure and as good as the poteen is. Just stop for a moment and consider the utter devastation that could occur in your life if you weaken your resolve and try poteen. Don't do it. Moreover, not all poteen on sale is the **'Real Stuff** '. As in any market there are criminal elements out to make quick, easy money and have no conscience about the harm they inflict. Making poteen is a traditional craft and art that requires time, care and one's full attention to get right. There are some blackguards who will add anything and everything to their poison just to take your money. Beware, It is poison! If you want the genuine poteen go to a trusted source of supply and you will enjoy it.

The tourists come to Ireland, and thank God for them. But, they wander around such tourist traps like Blarney, Bunratty, Killarney and such like believing this is the real Ireland. At these sites you find the usual attractions and goods seeking the tourist to spend their money on anything that might be associated with Ireland. Nowadays they have took to displaying beautifully labeled bottles marked "Genuine Irish Poteen." But do not be fooled. The only difference between them and any bottle of Irish Whisky is the color. You will know the genuine thing when you taste it and catch a hint of the turf fire that heated the still, as well as the smell of the heather from the bog land in which the still is hidden from view. There are, however, some producers who have given in to modern demands and made variations of their product. For ladies who may prefer a sweet taste to their drink some producers add lemon drop sweets, or brandy balls, and even cinnamon sweets specifically to cater for this market. Quite simply they add a number of these sweets to the basic bottle of poteen and allow them to dissolve in the clear,potent, liquid. The sweets add color and sweetness to the taste but most men do not need to be enticed by sweet flavors, though some may.

Finally most, if not all, alcoholic beverages carry a warning to the drinker, telling them to be " Drinkaware." This warning also applies to Poteen, though not printed on the bottle. There is, however, one additional warning that simply request that you do not allow even one drop of poteen to fall upon any highly polished furniture, metallic item, or even on any clothing that you wish to preserve. The liquid might look like water, but it definitely is not and should be handled only with the greatest care.

And now I have said my piece and have done honor to the beverage of my native land I lift my "Parting Glass" filled with poteen and wish all of you the best of Irish luck. Slainte (Irish for "Cheers").

When the Wind Blows

We ended the last section with a warning to all readers, but on this occasion we shall begin with a warning. The subject upon which I wish to speak now is not exactly to everyone's taste, and for this I must apologize. There are many subjects which are sometimes better not discussed because they tend to offend. This particular subject matter, however, is one that needs to be brought into the open and considered in depth. My mind was focused on the problem last Sunday morning at Church, as I was kneeling down to pray with all the members of the congregation. The Church itself was packed with people because it was a particularly important day for our Parish, every pew was filled to capacity. During our service we have a particular section called

"Prayers of the Faithful", which includes prayers for those members of our community who have recently died. The celebrant sets aside a period of silence in which we are to remember those members of our own family who have passed on from this life. People were crowding in and around me as we knelt in silence, meditating on all those loved ones who had departed. It was at that most inopportune moment that I heard a familiar ripping sound that foretells of a forthcoming attack on your nasal senses. In simple terms it was the sound of some person who had broken wind, and it certainly was not me.

I know it is easy to deny something like that in a crowd of people, but I can assure you I am being truthful. Naturally, I looked around my neighbors to see if there was any clue as to whom the perpetrator might be. The problem in this strategy is that quite a number of people were doing the same thing, and you have to make sure that you give then nothing that might cause them to suspect you. It was as I was glancing at my neighbors in the seat that I heard that familiar sound repeated. This time I was certain that the origin was somewhere in the pew in front of me. When I looked there, however, there were only three old ladies kneeling and apparently deep in prayer. This fact caused me to consider that, maybe, my ears were playing tricks on me. I looked at the person next to me and he nodded toward the three old ladies, which confirmed my own suspicions.

Just as I received this confirmation from my neighbor I noticed some movement in front of me. Two of the elderly ladies nervously shuffled sideways from the companion, who was kneeling between them. By making such a movement the ladies in front had helped pin-point the person responsible. It was still, however, quite difficult to grasp that a well-dressed elderly lady could emit such a foul odor. The smell that had already caused the old lady's two companions to attempt a discreet escape, and now the full strength of the stench reached me. Let me assure you, the reader, the aroma that old woman liberated was so thick you could have cut it with a knife. But once the smell hit your nasal organs the first task was to wipe the tears from your stinging eyes. I began to wonder what a person could eat that would cause such a smell to be concocted in their bowel, and then be freed in a rip of wind.

As I wiped the tears from my eyes I began to realize that several of my neighbors were looking at me in a rather accusing manner. There was now a sense of panic seized my body and I began to shake my head in denial, while simultaneously attempting to point out the real culprit with my eyes. But all around I could see mothers angrily nudge their children, and wives gave their spouses a dig in the ribs with their elbows. It dawned on me that I was not the only suspect and that I could only influence those immediately around me with my gestures. If the smell had penetrated further into the building then people in several rows behind me would also have been affected by its toxicity. They, however, could not see my silent pleas of innocence and I am sure that at least some of those people thought that I was the guilty party. Some of those closer to me could not quite believe my suggestion that the old lady was to blame. You cannot really blame them because, when it comes to it, what kind of person would accuse a well dressed, elderly lady of such a foul deed. In such circumstances what can an innocent man actually do? The lady did not admit to her act, nor did she offer any kind of apology for the deed.

Now I consider myself to be a tolerant type of person and there is not a male chauvinist bone in my body. Moreover, I quite understand that any person can suffer from flatulence, but it does appear to terribly afflict the female population in particular. The readers will recall that I have assured them that this observation is not part of any male agenda, but I am certain that you will agree that men approach the subject rather differently. It has been my experience that men do not look down upon those people who may have a weakness for flatulence, rather they accept that flatulence is simply another natural bodily function. Women, though, generally have a different reaction to this particular function of the body.

Do you ever wonder why the female sex do not accept flatulence in the same way as their male counterparts? The occurrence of flatulence in the female body is equal in numbers to that within the male body, but the female reacts very differently. They seem to believe that if they can avoid bringing attention to the act, or at least ignore it when it occurs, then none but the guilty will know from where the smell originates. But, more than this, it has been my experience that they will, in fact, go to great lengths to throw the more suspicious among us off their track. On many occasions I have seen ladies who immediately express surprise when they have broken wind by quietly uttering, "Oops!". They never seem to accept it with an "I apologize," "I am sorry," or an "Excuse me." Instead they choose to express surprise and it is my opinion that they do this not because it came upon them suddenly, but because they were surprised that it was accompanied by a noise. Furthermore, under certain circumstances, I have seen the female perpetrator reach around to their posterior once the wind has blown. I have often wondered if they are trying to muffle the sound, or are they really trying to put it back in as quickly as possible before the gas expands. Do these ladies not realize that once the wind blows there is no means of stopping it, or reducing its strength. When it is out, it is out!

With the growth in the incidence of IBS (Irritable Bowel Syndrome) flatulence appears to have become more common than previously was the case. Though the bodily function may be becoming more common it is still unacceptable for people to perform in public or before ladies. Before I proceed I wish to make it clear that IBS is an unfortunate and extremely uncomfortable medical condition. I very much sympathise with all those who have had to suffer from it. But there appears to be a growing number of people who choose to use IBS as an excuse for their inappropriate behavior. Unfortunately, there have been an increasing number of occasions when my wife and I have been confronted with extra strong, aromatic flatulence in restaurants, theaters and cinemas. On every occasion, however, the guilty person tries to fob us off with the excuse, "I have IBS."

While it is possible for me to appreciate and empathize with those problems that sufferers have, genuine patients are given ample advice on diet and medication to ease their difficulties. Even I can understand why Strong Curry and Hot Chilli are certainly never part of a suggested diet plan for IBS sufferers. We see people in a variety of establishments who insist on eating spice-filled dishes; or we see people in the cinema stuffing their faces with cheesy nachos, or hotdogs with fried onions, ketchup and mustard. When they finish eating they may feel a little bloated and decide to relieve themselves by simply "farting". Then, when their action proves to be louder than they expected it to be, and the aroma begins to hang in a cloud around them, they smile shyly and try to make you believe that they have IBS. Do they honestly think that we believe them?

Is this habit of not claiming responsibility just another sign of the general malaise in our modern society, where no person wants to be held accountable for their actions. My parents raised me to think differently; to consider that in the vast majority of cases honesty is the best policy. This means we should not commit any act for which we are not prepared to accept responsibility for the results of that action. In the context of this particular discussion it means, when flatulence suddenly comes upon you and is totally unavoidable immediately state, "Excuse me," or "Pardon Me." If you are not prepared to do this simple thing then I suggest that you evacuate yourself to an appropriate place where your exhaust and its fumes do not cause your neighbors difficulty or embarrassment. By accepting responsibility for your body's natural functions you will be playing your part in ensuring that the innocent remain innocent, and are never accused in the wrong.

At this stage of my discourse I must bring attention to those individuals who enjoy employing 'guerrilla tactics' in evacuating gas from their bowels. These are members of the SBD Group (Silent But Deadly Brigade) and it is virtually impossible to determine the source of their type of farts. These culprits take particular delight in settling themselves in small crowded places like a hall or an elevator, or more devilishly on an escalator, where they allow their body to evacuate stored wind. There is no accompanying noise to warn anyone that a fart has been released. This particular fart is a simple rush of warm wind expelled through the exhaust outlet without interrupting the 'baffles'. It is this fact alone which is the reason why this act is so diabolical. Records show that the aroma from one of these farts is of a particularly noxious, choking type that has a nasty tendency to linger for a considerable period of time, catching the unwary by surprise with no means of escaping the consequences. Often those who launch such farts will quickly regret their action because the smell can cling and they become concerned that the aroma will penetrate the fibers of their clothing. Selfishly, they worry that the smell will be around them the rest of the day and give no thought to the innocent bystanders caught in their foul deed.

Causing a smell in their clothes is a very light consequence for those who carry out these attacks. The most serious consequences for these people are "The Smeared Toga Result" or "The Skid Mark Result." Those dastardly personages who delight in launching these silent farts are very vulnerable to such consequences, which are usually a result of the "A Push Too Far Syndrome". They find a suitable site to launch an attack, such as an elevator, and let one go. There is the usual rush of warm air through the exhaust but, just as a sly smile breaks their lips, they feel the warmth turn to a cool dampness in the rear of their underwear. Panic sets in as the smell grows and the perpetrator knows that they have "pushed too far." They are obliged to make a quick exit to the nearest rest area, where they will have to do the best they can to clean themselves up. I have also seen such consequences befall those jokers who are best described as "Finger Pullers", "Leg Lifters ", and "Bum Cheek Raisers."

We are said to be living in an advanced technological society and yet the innocent are still left to suffer the consequences of another person's rash evacuation of wind from the bowel. Thankfully we have fire alarms, smoke alarms, gas alarms and even radiation alarms. It puzzles me as to why we have not developed some system that would alert us to farts, whether silent or noisy. Such an alarm does not have to be armed with loud sirens, red flashing lights, or whatever. Maybe it could just be a flashing LED light on a ring or a watch; maybe it could vibrate to give us ample warning of the approach of a foul smell. This may allow us to make adequate preparations for defense. There may even be room for some sort of direction indicator that could identify the source of the attack. As a recent victim of just such an attack I plead with all scientists to help bring an end to our suffering.... Meanwhile, let me leave you with the following warning -

STANDARD WARNING - PLEASE TAKE NOTE

1. For reasons of safety always take these precautions when farting
2. Always fart in a well ventilated room, away from children or pets.
3. Never fart near a naked flame, or attempt to ignite a fart.
4. Under no circumstances should you fart whilst suffering from diarrhoea or any similar medical condition. If in doubt consult your doctor.
5. **Never hold a fart in - it could make your heart explode.**

JAMESY

Jamesy Kelly had always been a young man who enjoyed his life to the full, and not in a bad way. From the day he was given his first bicycle he enjoyed speed and the thrill of the chase. But motorbikes were not the only things that Jamesy enjoyed. He played Gaelic football, Hurling and Soccer on a regular basis. Twice a week he took some of the local boys and trained them in the skills of Gaelic Football. So good were his junior teams that they won many awards, cups and medals. From Monday to Friday though, Jamesy drove a white "Mercedes" Van delivering varous items to homes and businesses throughout the area. The hours could be long and the work could be heavy going, especially in winter. But, Jamesy loved his job, often saying that the best thing about his job was that he met so many different people every day. His customers came from every walk of life and he had built up good contacts with many of the business people in the area. It was a job that suited Jamesy to the ground because he was outdoors and involved in driving a motor vehicle.

Marrying his wife, Greta, was the best day in his life and the best choice that he ever made. At least this is what Jamesy would tell everyone. The second best day in his life, Jamesy insisted, was the day that Greta gave birth to their only child, a son, who was considered to be the image of his father. Proudly this boy, named

Kevin by his mother and father, soared through his primary education and received much praise from his teachers for his intelligence. But what made Kevin popular among the people of the village was his lively personality and bright outlook on life. Many agreed that Kevin, like his father, had a smile that could brighten up a dark room, and the sound of his laughter would cheer up even the wettest of days. He was a good son and both parents doted on the boy, worshipping every step he took. They absolutely adored the very bones of their child and they were blind to any faults that he may have had.

Those who knew Greta saw in her the personality of a woman that was typical of an Irish Colleen. When she was a young woman she had fallen in love with Jamesy almost from the very first moment she had met him. That was a Sunday evening in the local dance hall and he had asked her to dance with him. Greta had known Jamesy before that night but only as an acquaintance to whom she could say "Hello." That first dance was followed by another and they spent the rest of the evening together. Jamesy walked Greta home after the dance, and they shared their first kiss. Within the year the couple were engaged, married and living in a house of their own.

Greta was very proud of the home that she had put together for Jamesy, and the beautiful, healthy son she was able to give him. There was no doubt that they had a beautiful home, filled with all the modern conveniences, but Greta preferred that her house looked like a home and not something taken from the pages of "Beautiful Homes" magazine. She may have preferred the lived-in look, but she was a house proud Irish mother and was constantly cleaning and tidying around the two men in her life. Meanwhile, the young and lively Jamesy Kelly had become the ideal domesticated married man thanks to the efforts of his wife. Greta had him well house-trained in proper protocols, at least the ones she thought were important. These included Jamesy leaving his dirty shoes in the hall, wearing slippers when in the house, and leaving the toilet seat down after he had used it.

They were not too long married, and yet, Jamesy was already only too well aware from experience, what even the smallest infringement of Greta's protocols could mean. Jamesy did not want to bring a storm of verbal abuse upon himself. Greta might be petite and gently spoken, but when riled she could have a tongue like a Cobra, quick and nasty. Jamesy preferred not to subject himself to any of Greta's bile, and he did not want to provoke her. He knew how, even on those occasions when something accidental happened, Greta could quickly become a domestic nightmare in which she was "all picture and no sound." At the same time, Jamesy knew that he was not a saint when it came to having patience.

Sport was big part of Jamesy's life and he took the local minor football team for training two nights every week. He would run the laps of the field with them, sprint with them and practice passing exercises with them. He enjoyed every minute he spent with those boys and, when he reached the age, Kevin was encouraged to join the club. Every Sunday afternoon, whether playing at home or away, Jamesy would be with the team coaching them as they played the game against the opponents. He pointed out strategy, organized the team and, on away days, organized the fathers to provide transport. At home games, however, Jamesy had the added benefit of being able to visit the club bar before and after the match. In the bar he could meet up with friends, talk tactics and discuss the game. At the same time, over a pint or two of "Guinness", Jamesy could share a joke, catch up on gossip and, generally, have a good time.

One of the things that Jamesy enjoyed most about these times was the 'banter' and the arguments that would arise. There were always those in the football club who were all convinced that they knew more than Jamesy did, and could do a better job. But, when it came to proving it by volunteering to coach the boys, only Jamesy and a few die-hard club members stepped forward. In the bar debates and arguments it was Jamesy's so called critics who soon found that he was more than a match for them. There was never any real bitterness or viciousness in those debates and arguments, for it was more like a group of boys getting together and playing a game of "Oneupmanship", by scoring points off one another.

Generally, Jamesy Kelly lived his life quietly now, keeping it simple and uncomplicated. Most days, after work. Jamesy would go straight home where he would eat his evening meal with Greta and Kevin. This was all precious time for Jamesy, who used it to catch up on the day's events and spend some time with the two most important people in his life. After the evening meal Jamesy would make his way to the Sport and Social Club, where he would have one or two pints of the "Black-Stuff". He would not have been recognized as a heavy drinker and tended to stick to the 'Porter' rather indulge in the whisky or other liquors. Then, every Tuesday and Thursday, he would take the young lads for minor football training come rain, hail or shine.

Jamesy detested the winter and the great chill that swept over the land. There was no Gaelic football matches and, therefore, no training. As Christmas approached the days got shorter, but Jamesy's hours of work always increased. The parcels and packages grew in number, size and weight, taking much longer to deliver. Some nights when he got home from work he found Greta had his meal in the oven and Kevin was gone to bed. Greta would sit with him while he ate, but Kevin's absence and Jamesy's fatigue lowered the quality of their precious family time. There were nights also when he was home so late, and he was so tired, that he did make his way to the club for a drink. On those nights it was better just to go to bed early and get as much rest as possible before rising the next morning to go to work.

One very cold December morning the Kelly household woke as usual at six-thirty. Jamesy rolled out of bed and pulled back the curtains to be greeted with the sight of an extremely heavy snowfall. He had not had a good night's sleep. His throat was sore, his nasal passages seemed block, and he was suffering from a cold sweat. Jamesy knew that it was probably the beginning of influenza and prepared himself for several days of suffering that undoubtedly lay ahead. "You may get up, Greta," he called to his wife. "The snow is lying thick on the ground, and it looks like there's more to come."

"I'm up, Jamesy" she replied, stretching her full length under the heavy duvet. "Will you make a wee cup of tea, While I get a wash and a shave?" he asked her.

"I will, and I will call Kevin," Greta told him.

Jamesy made his way to the bathroom on the landing and began his normal morning ablutions. Meanwhile, Greta pulled on her fleece dressing-gown and made her way downstairs to put on the kettle and make a pot of tea.

By seven-thirty Jamesy had washed and breakfasted. He lifted his car keys and moved into the hall to get his coat before going out of the front door. Buttoning his heavy jacket Jamesy turned to open the front door and found that the snow was lying about twelve inches thick on the ground. "Jesus, Greta the snow is a foot thick already," he called up to his wife who was still upstairs getting herself ready for her own work. "You will need to be extra careful when driving this morning. The roads will be bad," he warned her. "These back roads will not be salted or gritted."

"You need to be careful, too!" Greta responded.

"I drive these roads every day and in all weathers, you don't," he laughed. "I will see you about six tonight sweetheart."

"O.K., See you later," Greta replied as she finished brushing her hair in the bedroom mirror.

Jamesy went out the front door into the snow, closing the door behind him. The whole place was a mass of white snow and his car was totally covered with the ice-cold stuff. His feet crunched the snow beneath his boots as he walked to the car and began to remove the snow from the roof, windows and bonnet. It was by no means an easy task. Because the temperature had fallen so low during the night the bottom layers of snow had frozen to the glass of the car windows. He opened the car door and switched on the car's engine and the heater, focusing its warmth on the windscreens front and rear. Jamesy also reached over to the passenger seat and lifted the can of de-icer he had bought the previous day in anticipation of bad weather. The amount of snow that had to be removed before he could think of driving off to work, took Jamesy a good ten minutes to complete. His task finished he then clambered into the driver's seat of the car and was grateful to feel the warmth of the car's heater spread throughout the vehicle. Throwing the de-icer can back on to the passenger seat, Jamesy secured his seat-belt and adjusted his mirror. Putting the car into first gear Jamesy released the handbrake and steered the vehicle slowly through the gate. Ensuring there was no on-coming traffic, Jamesy finally pulled out on to the main road and drove off toward his work..

Inside the house Greta was putting the finishing touches to her make-up. It didn't matter how busy things were or how late she was, there was absolutely no way that Greta would leave the house until her make-up was perfect. A bit of lipstick and quick squeeze of "Eternity" here and there signaled the fact that she thought everything was now in place. "Are you ready yet, Kevin?" she called downstairs to her son, who was in the kitchen.

"Just finishing my breakfast," Kevin told her. "I'll be ready in a minute or two."

"Two minutes," Greta answered. "I can't afford to be late today."

Kevin looked at the clock in the kitchen and shrugged his shoulders. It was just gone eight o'clock and she didn't start work until nine. He knew from previous experience that his mother would be at least another ten minutes, for she rarely if ever left the house before quarter-past eight. He returned to his breakfast bowl and tucked into the last few spoonfuls of "Cornflakes" and milk that were sitting at the bottom. Given the opportunity Kevin would tell you that this was his favorite part of his regular breakfast ritual. With spoon in hand Kevin fished out the last milk sodden flakes before he finally raised the bowl to his mouth to slurp down the last of the milk. This was the choicest part of the breakfast for the milk had been sweetened by the copious amounts of granulated sugar that he had sprinkled over the "Cornflakes" before adding the milk. Moreover, it was warm milk rather than cold and it always gave him the perfect start to his day.

Suitably refreshed, and with his morning ritual complete, Kevin lifted his school uniform jacket from the back of the chair. Taking the jacket and his school scarf wrapped snugly around his neck. He could hear the thump of his mother's high heel shoes on the carpeted landing floor and reached for his school satchel, which sat in the hallway.

"Are you ready, Kevin?" Greta asked from the top of the stairs.

"I've been ready that long I could have grown a beard!" he replied cheekily.

Greta laughed and then chided him, "Not very funny, young man!"

"I thought it was," laughed Kevin.

"You should be on the stage. It left ten minutes ago," replied Greta sarcastically.

Kevin laughed and, as his mother reached the bottom of the stairs, he opened the door. Greta gave herself one last quick inspection in the hall mirror and then made her way out of the door, followed by her son. As she moved out into the cold, snowy morning Greta put on her overcoat, adjusting the fur collar to ensure her neck was adequately protected from the chill. "Start you on the passenger side," she directed Kevin as she began to clear the snow covering the driver's side of the car. With the two of them working together to remove the snow it did not take them long to clear the car, and have it ready to drive away.

Greta climbed into the driver's seat while Kevin, opening the passenger door, clambered into the passenger seat and secured his seat-belt. With both seat-belts securely fastened, and the rear mirror adjusted, Greta started the engine and steered the car out of the gate. She edged out on to the main road and then began to drive toward the village. The first stop on her way to work, every morning, was the school gate where she would drop off Kevin. He would always give her a peck on the cheek before he exited the car and said, "Goodbye." Then, as Kevin passed through the school gates, Greta would pull out into the traffic and drive straight to her job as a cashier in the local supermarket.

Kevin was now safely delivered to school and Greta shifted into first gear and was ready to pull out into traffic. She lifted her foot off the clutch, but to brake hard as an ambulance rushed past, sirens blaring and lights flashing. It was such a shock to her that her heart almost burst out of her chest and, in her panic, she stalled the engine. Greta took a long, deep breath and blessed herself quickly, thanking God she had not caused an accident. She started the engine again and muttered a quiet prayer for whomsoever the ambulance was rushing to treat. Turning toward the school gate once more she saw Kevin still standing there, shaking his head and mouthing toward her, "Be Careful." Greta smiled, waved at him and pulled out to continue her journey to work.

* * *

The ambulance sped through the village, spraying slush all over the footpaths, and two miles outside of the village it came to a halt with a slight skid. The snow was beginning to fall again lightly, threatening to add to the danger of the already hazardous roads. Due more to luck than judgement the ambulance driver had brought his vehicle to a halt only inches from a police car that was parked on the grass verge, all lights flashing as a warning to oncoming traffic. Fortunately traffic seemed to be very light on this particularly narrow B-road and the ambulancemen were able to gather what they needed without much delay.

"Good God" gasped the ambulance driver as they looked toward the scene of the reported accident. The snow was now thickening as it fell, piling more of its icy, white flakes on the wreck lying at the bottom of the ditch. There were already two police officers at the scene inspecting the vehicle and checking on the car's occupant. It was clear to the two ambulance men that the police officers needed their assistance as quickly as possible, and they carefully made their way down the steep side of the ditch.

The two police officers had tried their best to reach the driver of the vehicle, who was still in the car and unconscious. But such was the difficulty of the terrain and the severity of the snowfall that they could do very little. Their chances of being able to rescue the driver had now improved with the arrival of the ambulance personnel. Those chances improved further as a large, red fire-engine pulled up on the other side of the police car, and several uniformed fire-fighters clambered out of the vehicle.

"Be careful making your way down here," the younger of the ambulance men called up to the fire personnel.

"No problem," came their answer as the two ambulance men now made their way to the wrecked car. "What's happening?" they asked the police officers.

"Car doors are too battered to be opened by us and we cannot get to the driver, but it might be too late anyway."

"The fire men will have the proper equipment," the ambulance driver assured them and looked back to see what progress the fire men were making. Three of the fire men were already at the bottom of the steep bank of the ditch, while another two men were passing a large mechanical device to them. Meanwhile, one of the police officers and the young ambulance man were working hard at trying to gain entry to the vehicle through the badly smashed, toughened glass of the front windscreen. It was more difficult than they imagined it would have been, and they were glad to hear the approach of the fire men and the cutting gear. Trailing behind them in the snow all the way to the red fire-engine was a pneumatic hose. Now that they had reached the car they began to use the heavy metal device to cut an access to the car. Even as the machine began to work noisily to free him the driver still did not respond. "I don't think there is much need to hurry now," said the youngest ambulanceman. "The airbag has deployed correctly, but it didn't seem to do this guy much good."

Everyone had to stand back and allow the rescue workers to do their job. It took them a considerable amount of time to finally get access to the driver. When this was achieved the two ambulance medics swept into action, removing the unconscious driver and carefully laying him upon a stretcher. They began to assess the victim's condition, but it was quickly obvious that the poor man was indeed dead. The findings were confirmed by both medics and they gave their report to the senior police officer. Pressing the button on his personal radio the police officer spoke to the person at police control, "The victim of the RTA (Road Traffic Accident) has been confirmed as deceased. Have you had any luck with identifying the owner of the vehicle?"

Control immediately answered, "It has just come through from vehicle records."

"Who is it?"

""It appears the vehicle belonged to a Mr. James Kelly, with an address not far from the scene of the accident."

"That tallies with information from the driver's personal affects, "the senior police officer replied. "I think you had better organise family liaison officers to inform Mr. Kelly's next of kin." He sighed and then added, "To be honest, I don't relish their job."

WINGNUT

The village of Ardcraig is a small place in which very little happens and where every person knows everyone else. While most of these people were called by proper Christian names there were some inhabitants who were known by familiar names given to them by friends, and other villagers. So, if a person was to enter the village and ask the whereabouts of a man called James Joseph Molloy they would probably be met with blank stares. If that same stranger were, however, to ask the whereabouts of "Wingnut" then almost every person in the village would immediately know to whom he was referring. It may sound strange that a man would allow himself to be called "Wingnut". But Jimmy Joe had been called by this name since he was a child.

"Wingnut" was, I agree, a very odd name to give any child but it does demonstrate that very dry sense of humour for which the Irish have become known. The name "Wingnut" was actually more of a description of Jimmy Joe and, in all honesty, a very apt way to describe the man. Even as a young child he was tall for his age and as thin as a straw. Over the years this appearance changed very little and as he reached his mid-sixties he was still a tall, thin man. His completely bald head sat atop of his torso like the nut at the end of a bolt, and he had not one decent, healthy tooth in his mouth. But "Wingnut's" most outstanding features were, in fact, his large ears which stuck out several inches from each side of his shiny, bald pate. It was these that actually gave him the profile of the item after which he was named, namely a "Wingnut."

Jimmy Joe could never have been considered to be among the wealthiest or most influential of people in Ardcraig. He was, however, arguably the most well known character in the village. He lived in an old, dilapidated, thatched cottage nestled in the hills outside the village. To occupy him he worked a small parcel of land that consisted of such poor soil that it was fit only for rearing a few sheep and goats. These did not, of course, provide the old man with a huge income but he had a much more profitable product, which he produced in a hidden spot deeper among the hills. In a turf reek "Wingnut" had built himself an efficient Poteen still from which, many men in the village would tell you, came the best drop of "the Pure."

Unfortunately in our modern day Ireland there is little room left for the true subsistence farmer. Not so long ago there was a place for such men to raise a family and a make a basic living wage. But in these modern times the small farmer has been forced to make way for 'Big-time Agriculture' and farming estates. For the most part the small farmer has been forced to diversify while, at the same time, seeking paid employment in some other field of work This is, of course, the route taken by the industrious and "Wingnut" could never have been described as being an industrious type of person. The only area into which he was willing to diversify was one that didn't require too much work, and was illegal. It was, however, an industry into which he had been born. His father had trained him from an early age in the techniques for distilling top quality Poteen. Being illegal, of course, production and trade in Poteen was profitable though "Wingnut" never displayed his wealth. He could not have been described as being an osentatious person. "Wingnut" much preferred that people in the district thought of him as being simple-minded and poor. This was far from the truth.

The pitiful cottage in which "Wingnut" lived had been handed down from father to son over several generations and none seemed to have taken any great care in maintaining it. There was nothing special, or even quaint, about it. It was just a simple one floor cottage that looked much like any of the other white-washed, thatched cottages that were dotted all around the hills near Ardcraig. "Wingnut's" cottage did, however, reflect the level of poverty that he wanted to display to strangers and neighbours alike. He was quite unconcerned that his cottage differed from the majority of others in the area, in that its condition was a great deal inferior to them. The thatch on the roof was thinning in quite a few places, where it was beginning to rot and decay. That once rich, gold colour that the thickly thatched roof had possessed had now almost totally disappeared over the years because of a serious lack of attention. "Wingnut" had not put a white-wash brush to the walls of the cottage in many long years and they too had lost their colour. Rainwater constantly seeped through the rotting thatch, staining those cottage walls. The one thing that made the cottage distinctive was the manner in which, at very odd places and intervals, small, deeply-set windows were built into those discoloured walls. These small windows were not an efficient means of letting in light to the cottage interior. The shadow world was made worse by the fact that their small, square-shaped panes of glass had never seen a damp cloth that would make them clean again.

There was a narrow, rocky lane that led from the main road up to "Wingnut's" home which, when it rained, turned into a shallow stream of muddy water. Grass grew among the rock and, overall, it was hardly distinguishable from the poor, rock strewn land that it ran through. As you approached the cottage along that lane you could see, almost everywhere, groups of hungry looking sheep that stood bawling in various groups among the purple and white heather covered scrub land. In the Spring and Summer rains these heather bushes and gorse gave off a sweet aroma that filled the air with pleasant scents. Only the sorry state of "Wingnut's" home detracted from the raw beauty that this vista provided.

If you did not already know you could readily suspect that "Wingnut" had never married. It was clear from the condition in which his home was kept that it lacked the tenderness of a woman's touch. To look at the man in his mid-sixties it was quite easy to understand how members of the female gender preferred to avoid his company. He, of course, had his own personal reasons for remaining a single-man his entire life. After a few drinks with friends he would often tell them that he could never find a woman who was both sufficiently handsome, or sufficiently wealthy, to persuade him to marry them. There were other occasions when he would suggest that he had better looking goats than some of the single, eligible ladies who lived within a twenty-mile radius. "If you see two handsome looking women together in the Ardcraig area," he would joke, "they must be tourists." But, despite all his jokes, "Wingnut" was aware of the fact that the main obstacle standing in his way of gaining a wife was himself.

Jimmy Joe would never admit, even to himself, that he had any personal problems. There were many men who could count themselves as his friends, enjoyed his company and could tolerate his odd ways. Most women, however, shied away from him because his appearance and, indeed, many of them were frightened by him. His smile was not one that would capture the female heart. In fact "Wingnut's" smile could do more to frighten his sheep and goats than his dog's bark could. If he needed to gather in his animals from the hill sides all he would have had to do was smile at them and they would have stampeded back to the safety of the sheep pen.

Once "Wingnut" opened his mouth it was as if a mutated human was approaching, displaying black and green teeth, with breath like a cesspit. In their panic. One neighbour, who counted himself a friend, described "Wingnut" as being like a skull covered with a thin mask of rubber that was somewhat ill-fitting. In his big, wide mouth there was only one tooth that had anything like its former whiteness. The rest of them ranged in colour from dirty yellow to a drab, olive green, and finally black. The only real positive in all of this was that what teeth he had were very few in number and the white tooth that was left took pride of place at the front of the mouth like a signal lamp, attracting the full attention of an observer.

The one thing "Wingnut" could never have been accused of was being a "Dandy", or well dressed gentleman about town. It was not in his nature to dress to impress any person, no matter how important they were. Most of the time he wore a cotton shirt that, at one time, had been white but would have needed a good boil wash to return it to even a grey shade of white.For the most part it did not matter what colour his shirt was because over his shirt he wore an old boiler suit, which any normal person would have trouble stating, with any certainty, whether its original colour was blue or black. He would then, usually, accessorise this outfit with an old, heavy and worn tweed jacket which he would wear winter or summer. It was an item of clothing that was unusual because of the number of tears and holes that were in it. With all the makeshift repairs that had been made it was more like a patchwork quilt than a jacket. Some of his friends, at least for a time, took to calling him "Joseph and his Dream Coat" after the musical of that name. But of all his clothing items "Wingnut's" most outstanding features were his well-worn, green coloured rubber, knee length boots that he rarely removed from his feet.

"Wingnut's nearest neighbours were the O'Brien family, who lived about half a mile down the main road from the end of his farm lane. This family consisted of Mick and his two spinster sisters, Mary and Brigid, who maintained a small but very profitable farm. Mick O'Brien, like "Wingnut", was a man whose devotion to the single, unmarried life was unquestionable. He was, at this time, in his seventies and living a comfortable life being waited-on hand and foot by his two sour-faced sisters. They were a long established family in the area and over several generations had built a healthy, productive farm business. But, although Mick and his two sisters were people of some wealth none of them had ever attempted to cultivate any kind of serious relationship with a member of the opposite sex that may have ended in marriage. Mick O'Brien, for one, when he was a younger man had pursued relationships with several ladies in the Parish who had wanted this relationship to go much further. The entire idea of marriage, however, was something that Mick preferred to avoid at all costs. He wanted to enjoy all the comfort and romance that these relationships brought him, but he had no intention of "paying the bill". His two sisters, Mary and Brigid, had not been so fortunate to have as many romantic encounters in their lives. Sadly, for both women, they had never had any form of romantic experience with the exception of that which they read about in "Ireland's Own" and "The People's Friend."

Mary was most definitely the smaller and more genteel of the O'Brien sisters. She was the shy sister who preferred to stay hidden in the shadow of her two siblings. There were quite a few men in the district who could recall Mary as a young woman and had considered her, at the time, to be quite a beauty. Mary's father was considered to be a very protective man who would not even entertain the prospect of a local suitor being good enough to marry his daughter. There were, without doubt, many good men who could have provided well for Mary and given her healthy children to care for, but her father's criteria was such that no man could hope to gain his blessing. Even after her father had passed away Mary's brother, Mick, took up the mantle as head of the family and kept a firm control.Mary, for her part, was always reluctant to consider the possibility that she might actually encourage any man to admire her. To ensure that this would be the case she always dressed in the drabbest of clothes and contented herself in her role of caring for her siblings in the family home.

Mary's sister, Brigid, was a completely different 'kettle of fish'. She was as different in appearance and mannerisms from her sister as chalk is from cheese. As previously pointed out, Mary had never attempted to cultivate any kind of serious relationship with members of the opposite sex. The key word in her case being, "serious". From various reports, however, when Brigid was a young woman she sought the company of many young men and delighted in sharing favours with them in a variety of barns, hay sheds and ricks. In those days, it has been said, Brigid was keen to experiment but there would now be few of her male friends who would freely admit to have been her lover at any time. While she undoubtedly found enjoyment in the company of men she was never to find true romance, or the love that would win her a caring husband. Men, in general, are not very difficult creatures to understand. Young men, especially, have certain sexual yearnings that they need to fulfill and if they can do this without troubling their consciences too much that is all the better. Brigid O'Brien was a large woman who would never have won any prizes for her good looks. It was said that she never cared much for personal hygiene and that her breath was so bad it would have curdled milk if she blew on it. But such physical traits were not enough to cause eager young farming men to avoid her freely given favours, though the line was drawn at any idea of something more serious.

There was a time when Mick O'Brien had hopes that he might persuade "Wingnut" to show interest in his sister, Brigid. He and "Wingnut" had been friends since the time they were at school together. Jimmy Joe, however, had been one of the young farmers who had been enjoying Brigid's free favours and, at the same time, there was some concern in the O'Brien household that Brigid was pregnant to some local boy. Mick was fully aware that his friend was not 'the sharpest knife in the drawer' but neither was he a total fool. "Wingnut" would never have been considered a prize catch for any family's daughter, but even he was not prepared to spend the rest of his life with the likes of Brigid O'Brien. In the end Mick was not offended, or even surprised, at "Wingnut's" lack of interest in his sister even when her pregnancy scare was proved to be without foundation.

Both "Wingnut" and Mick considered themselves to be connoisseurs of poteen. There was nothing that the two men liked more than to down a glass, or several, of the 'Pure Drop.' Mick O'Brien fully appreciated his friend's ability to manufacture a good batch of poteen and, as a good friend, he was always available to help him test the quality of the product by tasting it. Almost every Saturday evening, after he had attended to his animals, Mick would take a stroll up the road towards "Wingnut's" cottage. The building may have appeared to be dilapidated and in need of some repair, but any visitor to the cottage could be assured of a warm welcome. Mick took his usual seat at a round wooden table that was usually littered with an assortment of dirty cups and plates. "Wingnut" would usually clear these away into the sink before putting a bottle of poteen in the centre of the table, accompanied by a couple of dusty glasses. A quick blow into each glass would clear most of the dust from the glasses allowing "Wingnut" to pour out the poteen and talk with his friend about the events of the previous week in Ardcraig.

"Wingnut" always maintained a good fire in the old, blackened stone hearth, which radiated light as well as heat. The gloom of the cottage's interior was further illuminated by a couple of oil-filled, hurricane lamps strategically placed in the room. There never had been either gas or electricity piped into this old cottage, and "Wingnut" had never seen or enjoyed the benefits of such utilities in his home. The fire gave him warmth. The hurricane lamps gave him light, while a wood burning range gave the ability to cook whatever food he chose to eat. With a bottle of poteen on the table and sufficient light to pour it by everything was ready for socialising. Both men relaxed at the table by the blazing turf fire, drinking the strong clear liquid and there they sat until the early hours of the morning. Finally, when Mick had decided he had taken enough refreshment, he made his excuses to Jimmy Joe and staggered home to his bed.

Early every Sunday morning Mick O'Brien, Mary and Brigid would leave their cottage and walk the two miles to Mass in the village. "Wingnut", walking on his own, usually caught up with his friend and neighbour a little bit down the road, and together they would walk toward Ardcraig. It was a regular sight to see all four processing along the narrow country road until they eventually reached the small, grey-granite Church dedicated to St. Kevin. Mick and "Wingnut" would walk together talking about sheep and the prices that they might receive at market, as well as a wide-range of other farming subjects. Meanwhile Mary and Brigid walked a few yards ahead of the two men, gossiping about the people they might meet at Church, the news they might hear, and the updates they might receive. It was the weekly trip to Mass that would provide the two busy-bodies with all the news they required to fill their hours of talk during the rest of the week. Each sister had their own circle of informants to question and their greatest pleasure was spending their own leisure time comparing the stories that they had been told.

The first task that faced the four neighbours each Sunday morning, however, was to make their way to Father Halpin's Mass irrespective of what weather faced them. In the Church and seated they would have to listen to an unnecessarily long and angry homily against sin, which seemed to last forever. But, while Father Halpin berated his congregation, Mick and "Wingnut" sat their weary bodies at the back of the Church taking advantage of the chance to catch up on lost sleep and recuperating from their self-inflicted hang-overs from the previous night. The two sisters were not so lucky. They always sat at the front of the Church and could only suffer Father Halpin's homily quietly offering up their suffering as a penance for any future sins they might be tempted into committing.

On the feast of Saint Patrick the Parish of Ardcraig held special celebrations that always began with a Mass, celebrated in the Irish language by Father Halpin. It was probably only one of three Masses held in the village each year that the Parish Priest could be sure the entire Catholic population would attend; the other two Masses being to celebrate Easter and Christmas. As soon as Father Halpin said the words, "Go the Mass is ended", it was if he had blown the whistle at the end of a football match. The entire assembly of men, women and children hurried out of the Church to join in the special celebrations that local businessmen and organisations had especially arranged for the day. In the village school grounds a garden fete had been set up, at which there were a variety of stalls selling a great number of goods. There were handicraft items for sale, games of chance to be played, and tombola prizes to be won. The money that the village raised from all these things was always donated to various Parish charitable groups and purposes. At the same time, in the school hall, groups of local women served tea and cakes as part of their contribution to the celebrations, while other groups of ladies prepared and cooked large pots of Irish Stew and buttered Soda-Bread for the lunch time rush that would come when the public houses closed for a couple of hours.

Dinny Keegan's public house, in particular, was the most popular public house in the entire Ardcraig district. Not surprisingly it was to Keegan's Pub that most of the male population of the village went to after Mass. Every Saint Patrick's Day Keegan's Pub would fill up quite rapidly, causing Dinny and his staff to work almost non-stop to serve the stout and whisky ordered by their customers. Father Halpin, being the Parish Priest, was a cautious man and managed to avoid the prying eyes of the village gossips by entering Dinny Keegan's kitchen in order to "wet the shamrock" privately. But, as the clock in the bar chimed one o'clock, Dinny would close his inn and watch as the men of the village filed out of the main door in small groups, staggering on their way to the school yard and the school hall. Among this company there were always a few of the men who carried a bottle or two of stout in their pockets. There were others, also, who had already taken advantage of the opportunity to purchase a stock of "Wingnut's" best product.

There were several ladies in the village who also enjoyed spending a little time at Keegan's Pub and would squeeze themselves into the "Snug", where they could enjoy their drink in relative peace and quiet. But, once the clock chimed and the men began to leave, so too the women would exit the bar to follow them over to the school hall, where the feast was ready. This was a highlight of the day for the young of the village and they quickly ate up the free Irish Stew and Soda-bread. The adults also enjoyed this special part of the day though, instead of washing down their food with soft drinks, they chose to drink their beer, stout, whisky, and poteen.

Saint Patrick was known for depriving himself of any luxury and, perhaps, that is the reason that the Saint's feast day always fall within that period of spiritual preparation known as "Lent". For the Catholic community "Lent" is a time when they usually deprive themselves of some luxury and offer it as a penance before the arrival of Easter. In Ireland, however, the tradition has long been that the feast day of St. Patrick was a day given by God, to the Irish alone, when they could forego their Lenten abstinence without guilt. It does not take much for any Irish person to enjoy a celebration, but when "given" permission by God and Saint Patrick they take full advantage. Perhaps that is why so many people throughout the world suddenly "find" Irish roots in their family tree when it comes to 17th March. On this day they are permitted, apparently, to drink and feast until their hearts are content.

When the village clock struck three in the afternoon Dinny Keegan would open his hostelry doors once more to provide quality beverages. It came as no surprise to him when the first people to come through those doors were Mick O'Brien and Jimmy Joe Molloy. Outside the pub children were usually engaged in fancy dress parades, or demonstrated their Irish Dancing skills, or exhibited their musical prowess with violin, guitar, and bodhran (pronounced "Bowran" - an Irish style circular hand drum). By seven o'clock in the evening the outside entertainment was at an end. The less sturdy drinkers and party-goers of the village had decided that they should return home with their children. Meanwhile the public houses of Ardcraig continued to celebrate with Irish traditional music and Ceilidh dancing. "Wingnut" and Mick had no interest in dancing, of course, but they enjoyed the hospitality in Dinny Keegan's until it closed for the night. Just as you would expect these two men to be the first customers through the door, so too they were always the last to leave at closing time.

Mary and Brigid had, as usual, returned home earlier in the evening and when Dinny's doors closed on the night Mick and "Wingut" staggered homeward out of the village. The street lights ended at the village boundary, and the two men had to continue up the long, dark, country road that wound its way into the hills. It was a bitterly cold night to be walking home, which caused Mick and "Wingnut" to occasionally halt their progress in order to take another "Wee Nip" from the poteen bottle that "Wingnut" always carried with him. Stopping for a wee warming drink also gave the two friends to recall the humorous episodes that they had witnessed that day in the village. It also gave them a chance to joke with each other about the potential hangover they undoubtedly would have the next morning. Mick, however, on one occasion had a great need to relieve himself and he hurried to one side of the road, trying to open the zip on his trousers. He just made it in time and relieved himself into the hedge. He was also very fortunate that there was no car on the dark, unlit road to illuminate Mick's anti-social act. Mick, of course, did not care who seen him at the hedge for he believed that when you had to go you went.

Mick was right at the edge of the hedge that ran parallel to the verge of the road and separated it from a field of quietly ruminating cattle. "Wingnut", in the meantime, was singing loudly to himself in such a slurred manner that none but himself could understand what he was singing about. In fact, "Wingnut" had become so involved in his song that he neither heard nor saw the black coloured Volkswagen that came speeding around the corner. Just as Mick was trying desperately to zip up his trousers again he heard the screech of car brakes on the road, and a loud dull thump of a vehicle hitting something. Completely forgetting about his zip difficulties, Mick turned to see what had happened and caught a fleeting glimpse of the car. The engine revved hard and almost in a flash it sped off again toward the village. Looking across the road there was no sign of "Wingnut".

"Jesus! Wingnut?" he called out as he staggered to the place where he had last seen his friend standing. Mick's eyes, a little foggy from the poteen, did their best to scan the darkness for some sign of his friend. By some miracle Mick managed to distinguish something that was lying on the road about twenty yards from where he was standing.

"Ahh, Wingnut," Mick called out as he staggered toward the motionless object on the road and finally stopped as he reached the protrate body of his friend. The head of the body was on the road and his feet were buried into a thick clump of bramble bushes. Mick immediately knelt down beside the body and shook it, tearfully calling, "Wingnut?"

The head moved and the eyes opened, "Jesus Mick, I thought that bastard had killed me!"

PIG BUSINESS

Ireland in the years immediately following the end of World War Two was a much different society than it is today. There was a much more strict moral code in that society when it came to relations between men and women. But, at the same time, would look elsewhere when it came to shady business dealings. "One hand in your pocket and the other hand on the rosary beads," was one description of Ireland in those days.

The war had been good to a lot of so-called businessmen, especially those who smuggled goods across the border into British-controlled Northern Ireland. It was illegal, but it provided jobs and money for many small businessmen and their employees. Men like Phil McCracken were looked upon as almost "Robin Hood" figures by a lot of their neighbours and they chose to overlook any dubious business methods they may employ. In today's society men like McCracken would undoubtedly be exposed by the media for being what he was, namely a criminal and a scam artist. In those days, over sixty years ago, there were many who did business with Phil and would tell you that he was as honest as the day is long. Well, as honest as a professional smuggler can be.

Philip McCracken, known to most as "Wee Phil", was born and bred, and proud to be a native of Connaught. In local parlance he was considered to be a "Cute Hoor", or person who is well known among to be crafty in their business dealings. It could be said that being "Cute" is a trait that seems to be common among people from Connaught, many of whom were considered to be "tight-fisted". There is an old Irish adage that states "When you shake hands with a Connaught man make sure you check all your rings are still on your fingers before ensuring your money is still in your pocket." Smooth talking men could sell sand to the Arabs, always making sure it was damp so that it would weigh more. Be assured that "Wee Phil" was indeed the epitome of a man from that western province of Ireland.

"Wee Phil" was a well known pig farmer, who was also known as Philip. The father was a man who had brought himself up from nothing to be a leading farmer in the area. During this struggle he had learned quite a number of dubious, but successful, business methods which he carefully taught to his son. "Wee Phil' was only one of several children in the family, but he was the only one willing to follow in his father's footsteps. As soon as they were able to leave home they did so and moved on to "Greener Pastures". But, after his father had passed on, "Wee Phil" increased the size of his herd and extended the acreage of his land. The family home, however, never changed, remaining as it had in his father's day. Phil was definitely a wealthy man but he wasted none of his wealth on the house. It remained a simple, white-washed, two-storied building. At the side of the house there was an old loft, where hay and dry-feed was stored while, at the rear, was an old milking shed that was now empty and used to store several pieces of aging farm equipment. There was no sign of a woman's touch about the house and it was unlikely there ever would be. "Wee Phil" liked being a single man, which meant that he could spend all his time on improving his herd of pigs.

From the moment he began to walk and was able to help his father about the farm "Wee Phil" developed a passion for rearing pigs and for developing the breed. Over the years that he worked alongside his father soaking up every ounce of knowledge that the old man had gathered. At the same time, however, "Wee Phil" was open to employing new ideas and modern methods of pig production. So successful was he that from the age of fifteen years "Wee Phil" had built up an enviable reputation for himself in the Province for his pig management and breeding skills. Among his favourite pastimes was attending local livestock auctions and fairs, at which he learned the skills of a dealer. He took note of their methods, but he also took note of the various scams that some would put into action.

The McCracken Farm quickly became the largest pig producers in the West of Ireland. "Wee Phil's" reputation spread to all parts of the island and there were many pig-breeders who sought his advice. Unfortunately for these people "Wee Phil" was not free with his advice, but was as miserly with such advice as he was with his money. Moreover, those to whom he did give advice soon realised that he was duplicitous with this as he was with the majority of his business dealings. Some may have simply called him a "Chancer", but many more were convinced that he was an out and out cheat. Local dealers knew how Phil conducted his business and with them he usually played fair, though hard, in his dealings. Those outside the Province were never sure how much they could trust Phil when it came to business. Socially he could be a real gentleman, but in business he could be a real "Attila the Hun."

When it came to selling pigs Phil knew every trick in the book. He could "blind" people with science, or he could talk in such a way that he would appear to be just a simple country farmer. He could make an old pig look young, or poor ones to look fit and healthy. It was not that he told lies to people but rather did not tell them the whole truth. It was a matter of taking an old product, shining it up a little, and repackaging it to suit the particular requirements of a potential purchaser. Those who knew Phil also knew not to take what he told them at face value, but to read between the lines. His expression would never change, making it that much harder for a person to "read" him or his mood. That was, perhaps, his greatest asset in the world of business. Moreover, it helped convince those who did not know his ways that he was completely naive when it came to business. It was the perfect poker-face, betraying no emotion even when he had gained a victory over an opponent. At the same time, however, he had the sort of personality that would make purchasers and vendors feel that they had got one over on him, handing over their money or their goods to him almost with a smile on their faces.

There really was nothing humorous about "Wee Phil", but his appearance did cause some to chuckle quietly. He was a man who was small in stature, standing only four feet eleven inches tall. His waistline, however, was larger in proportion stretching a little over forty-six inches in circumference. There was a time in his youth when he did have a head of thick, glossy, red hair but those days were now long past, and what little hair was left was almost invisible against his skull because it was so grey. In fact, the only redness left to "Wee Phil" existed on his nose and his large, fat cheeks which stood out clearly against his pale white skin, that is a trait of people from the West of Ireland. They complemented Phil's thick lips and his large ears that some had compared to radar dishes sat on each side of his large, round head.

Phil McCracken definitely had money behind him, of that there was little doubt even though he looked as if he hadn't two pennies to rub together. He was one of those miserly people who believed that if people realised how much money he had then they would expect him to pay more for their goods. At the other end of the spectrum purchasers of his pigs may expect him to sell them at a lower price. By appearing to others as if he had "neither in or on him" Phil could disguise his wealth. There were few occasions, in fact, when "Wee Phil" didn't wear those same old, dusty, tan coloured brogues over thick woollen socks that had also seen much better days. Old, dark brown, patched corduroy trousers were his preferred attire and were held to his portly waistline by a long piece of green coloured bailing twine. Under an aged, frayed tweed jacket he wore a shirt made from cheap cotton that he always kept open at the neck, the collar of which badly needed washed. On his almost bald pate he wore a dilapidated, broad brimmed faded tan hat that protected his face from the sun. It was one of those second-hand treasures that he had picked up at the markets, along with an old, hessian, army satchel which he strung over his shoulders. Inside that bag, that he carried everywhere, he had placed a notebook, a lunch box of sandwiches and an old, rolled up, plastic raincoat. Even though he had absolutely no need for it, Phil walked with the aid of a "Blackthorn Stick". This he held in his right hand while in his left he held a long, coarse rope lead that was attached to a small, pot-belly pig he called "Archie" and kept as a pet.

At this time, the early 1950s, in Connaught many pig farmers kept their pigs in a free range environment rather than locking them up in sties. There were sties of course but these were normally used for farrowing and for housing the animals in winter. The pigs, because they had a freedom to roam, took full advantage of that freedom and wandered through the fields and farmyards. Sometimes, however, freedom of movement is just not sufficient to calm down an animal that is best described as a big, fat, ugly, bad-tempered and disobedient beast. Normally the pig struts around in an extremely haughty manner, or else simply lies down in the dirt to sleep, or munch greedily at its food. The only time when a pig can be said to be truly lively is when it is fighting other pigs over food, or is seeking the female of the species to satisfy its yearnings to breed. The term "Greedy Pig" is an apt description for all these animals rather than a select few. A pig may lie in the dirt, pretending to sleep, but it always keeps at least one eye open for food. Even though the farmer provides his pigs with food it is never enough for them and they will seek out new sources of supply by breaking into a store, for other foodstuffs.

Pigs, like most farm animals, care little about security or shelter when it comes to seeking out food. Because they are used to being free to roam it is not surprising that the fields, farmyards and farm enclosures quickly become too small for them. Their inquisitiveness soon gets the better of them and they may break out to wander the country lanes and roads. They root in the verges and fields of crops for any tasty morsels that they might find. These pigs, especially if unmarked, were viewed as fair game by "Wee Phil. Buying pigs was the mainstay of Phil's business, but he was not beyond gathering or "liberating" a few animals who may have appeared to have no known owner. Phil would argue that pigs which took to roaming country lanes and roads were unhappy pigs. He would say that they were unhappy with their current owner and keen to find a new owner who would look after them much better. "Wee Phil" truly believed that there was nothing dishonest or illegal about finding some of the "liberated" pigs and giving them a new home. If they were unmarked, or not tagged then they were orphans and entitled to the new home he could provide for them.

Being the businessman that he was, Phil McCracken was a firm believer in marking his property to ensure it did not go missing. Pig production was, and remains, big business in Ireland. As far as Phil was concerned it was vital to business survival that valuable property be marked so it could be returned to the rightful owner. But such marking should be of a permanent nature because anything temporary could be easily removed, which Phil knew from experience. There was an old saying that Phil always lived by and that was simply, "Finders Keepers, Losers Weepers." Phil, however, was rarely the loser.

Phil McCracken's story only gets interesting when one looks back on his father's efforts to improve the breed. Over thirty years previous to the beginning of our story "Wee Phil's" father found himself at a loose end when "The War of Independence" came to an end in Ireland. Phil senior had a great interest in pigs and for improving the more common breeds that farmers kept. His breeding experiments on his own small farm and this, he believed would make his fortune. The main goal for these experiments was simply to create a new, much leaner, more active, and disease resistant breed of pig. Phil senior's experiments began with him attempting to bring together the modern breed of pig with an old, very rare breed of Irish pig.

Four hundred years ago this ancient breed of pig was common in many places throughout Ireland, some of which were domesticated by the peasantry. These pigs, however, were a wild breed, lean and mean, active and very dangerous. The introduction of the more amenable modern pig breeds reduced their numbers in domestication because they were more docile and easier kept. Meanwhile, the wild "Irish Pig" became a heavily hunted animal by the peasantry and local gentry alike. But, the "Irish Pig" became almost extinct as a species with only a few remaining among the remotest, forested hills of Connaught. In more modern times those who have seen these animals have described them as being taller, longer-legged and more loose of limb than the domesticated pigs. Witnesses have told that the "Irish Pig" is very quick on its trotters and much more agile than the pigs most of us are used to seeing. They have been likened to a large, heavy-bodied greyhound with elegantly arched backs, short ears and faces that exhibited a higher level of animal intelligence.

Phil senior succeeded, after a time, in creating a hybrid pig whose meat was both leaner and tastier than that of the popular domesticated pig. Unfortunately the hybrid animals retained their great agility, bred more rapidly, and were virtually uncontrollable in the open. A lot more experimentation and money was put into trying to reduce the negative aspects of the breeding programme, but without success. They may have provided better pork products but, because they were uncontrollable, no sane person in Ireland wanted them. It was now up to "Wee Phil" to source a market for these pigs and recoup at least some of the money his father had invested in them. "Wee Phil" was very much aware that England was still suffering some shortages from the rationing that had been imposed during the war with Germany. At the same time there were a number of people keen to make a profit out of such circumstances and their greed might just bring Phil a good profit. It was an opportunity that "Wee Phil" could not ignore.

As a first step "Wee Phil" sprinkled a calming drug into the food that he fed to the hybrid pigs, before organising several workers to usher them into a transport lorry. He also prepared and cooked several pounds of the hybrid meat to use as samples and packing these into the lorry he drove to the docks in Dublin. There he would boarded the overnight ferry to Liverpool and during the crossing he was allowed access to the lorry to feed and water his "pigs", which included his pet pig "Archie". The feeding time gave Phil another opportunity to ensure his cargo was given a good dose of the sedative solution. It would be needed for the long journey to come, after they had docked in Liverpool.

The research that Phil had undertaken prior to leaving Ireland had highlighted Yorkshire as the most likely place to find a buyer for his cargo. He had also learned that Yorkshire men were also famed for being somewhat careful with their money, but he felt himself to be more than a match for any man when it came to dealing. With "Archie" restrained and secure in the cab of the lorry on the passenger seat, Phil drove the lorry from Liverpool docks and headed for the main route across the Pennines to Yorkshire. He used the time positively by considering very carefully the strategy that he would employ to entice potential purchasers to buy his pigs. Though he knew that there was a need for his herd of "Irish Pigs" he was determined that he would get the best price possible from men noted for their reluctance to pay the full price for anything. Phil's strategy would be simple and well tested. He would employ the tactic of "put on the poor mouth", pretending to be a simple Irish pig farmer who was unprepared for the worldly wise Yorkshire men. In the end they would, as others had done, give him their money with a smile that came from a belief that they had "got one over" on him. This, of course, had never been the case and it would be Phil who would be the one with the broadest smile.

The countryside of Yorkshire reminded Phil so much of his home county. He studied it as he drove along the country roads seeking potential customers for his pigs. It was not as easy a task as Phil had once thought it would be. It was just after midday when he noticed a small group of men in a nearby field, urging a group of about a dozen pigs toward the farmyard. Phil wasted no time in driving his lorry into the farm lane that led to a large house and yard. He pulled the lorry up to a stop just as the last of the squealing pigs were driven into a sty. At the head of the group of men stood a tall, well built, bearded man who, seeing Phil's lorry made his way toward the stranger. Meanwhile Phil could hear the growing noise of his cargo as the sedative began to wear off. This was a signal that warned him that a deal needed to be completed, sooner rather than later.

"Good day to you, Sir" the bearded man greeted Phil. "What can we do for you?"

Phil raised his hat slightly in response, "And a good day to you. Would you be the master?" He smiled shyly at the farmer and spoke in his broadest West of Ireland accent, giving the appearance of being a simple country yokel.

"I am," said the farmer. "Charles Emdyke is my name."

"Mr. Emdyke, your honour, I am glad to meet you," Phil smiled at him, bowing his head and putting two fingers to the brim of his hat as a sort of salute. "I have a herd of fine pigs to sell. They are all well -reared, with good lean meat that will melt in the mouth. I have some samples of prepared items with me for you to taste."

"I don't need any more pigs than I have," Mr. Emdyke told Phil, but he was not put off by his answer.

"Good Pig meat is hard to come by, but these are priced at a steal," Phil insisted.

"Sure there were only about a half dozen pigs driven into the sty," Phil pointed out by nodding his head over toward the sties. "There must be room for a lot more."

"Aye?" laughed the bearded farmer. "There is room for more, but no money to bargain with."

"Now, Mr. Emdyke, I have twelve top-grade Irish pigs the likes of which you have never seen . Give me your best price and see if we can make a deal," Phil told him as he climbed out of the lorry cab.

Mr. Emdyke stood and watched as Phil clambered out of the lorry cab and then told him, "But, I have no need for any more pigs."

Phil wouldn't allow such declarations to defeat his intentions. "The people are crying out for good pork products and I am giving you a great start in meeting these needs for very little money," he told Emdyke.

"Aye, there is a definite need for your pigs but I wouldn't have the money to buy them from you," Emdyke said. Phil was now getting the definite impression that Mr. Emdyke was becoming frustrated with the continuing efforts to close the sale. He returned to the lorry cab and retrieved some of the prepared produce for Mr. Emdyke to taste.

"It's great pork," he told Phil.

"Well how much would you expect to pay for meat like that?"

"More than I could afford," Emdyke sighed.

Wee Phil put on his broadest smile and asked, "How much would you be willing to pay?"

It was just what Emdyke wanted to hear. He turned his eyes heavenward and pretended to be considering a price that he thought the Irishman might accept. But as a starting gambit he told Phil, "I'm sure they might fetch twelve to fifteen a pig."

"Aye that would be good price, indeed," Phil told him. "If I was selling to a producer at the factory. To someone like you, a breeder, I was thinking maybe 10 pounds for each animal would be better."

"Ten pounds is a good price alright, but it is still a bit too rich for me," Emdyke replied.

"How much would be good for you?" asked Phil without any sign of urgency.

Emdyke, however, was a hardened dealer and answered immediately, "You'll not get me that way, Paddy. I do not need any more pigs"

Phil resented the way English people tended to call all Irishmen "Paddy", but he held his tongue on this occasion. " Of course you do," Phil insisted." You'll have them sold tomorrow at double the price and make a tidy profit." He saw the man's eyes light up with expectation, and decided it was time to close the "trap". "Give me one hundred pounds for all twelve in the back and I will throw in the fat, pot-belly pig in the cab. That one's an Irish champion and will fetch a good price."

You could see the cogs turning in the mind of the Yorkshire man and the pound signs totaling up in his imagination. It was a deal that he just could not turn down. Emdyke spat on his hand and offered it to Phil, "It's a deal!"

Phil didn't hesitate to take the man's hand to seal the bargain. "Sure I will put them into the sty for you, while you get the money."

"Two of my men will help you to move them."

"That's not really necessary," Phil told him. "But if you wish them to help then I will accept all the help you can give," he smiled.

Mr. Emdyke called two of his workers over to the lorry and told them to do whatever they were asked to do to unload the pigs from the lorry into the large sty. Take long for the task to be completed, which allowed Phil to release "Archie" and parade him in front of the farmer and his workers. "That's a sound animal you have there," Mr. Emdyke pointed out.

"It's a sound beast alright," Phil replied. "It is a special animal that is very highly strung. Just allow this champion pig to settle down in its new surroundings, perhaps you would tie it up in the garden. Just for tonight."

"We'll do that," replied Emdyke as he handed a wad of notes over to Phil. The two men shook hands and passed on their final greetings before they parted.

"Here is your receipt and proof of ownership," Phil told the farmer. "I thank you for your business and, should God spares us both, we will do business in the future."

Mr. Emdyke nodded his head in agreement and watched as Phil climbed into the cab of his lorry. The Irishman then drove his now empty lorry out of the farmyard and down the lane to the main road. As the lorry drove down the lane Emdyke turned to his workers and told them, "Get those pigs fed and locked up for the night. Tie this one up in the garden, while I go back to the office and make a few calls. There's big money to be made here." They all laughed loudly.

"He thought he was the smart one," said one of the workers, "but you got the better of him, Sir."

As Emdyke went toward his office "Archie" was taken by its rope lead to a concrete post in the rear garden of the house, tied up there, and was told that he would get fed later. The farmer then made his way into the house to make the phone calls to his contacts to get a good price for the pigs he now had in his sties. Meanwhile, a half mile down the road from the farm, Phil stopped the lorry and pulled it into the side of the road. Sitting behind the steering wheel Phil opened a newspaper and began to read. After what seemed to be about fifteen minutes Phil heard a familiar snorting sound and climbed down out of the lorry cab. Standing on the passenger side of the lorry was "Archie" and what remained of the rope lead that he had bitten through to gain his freedom. "Good pig, Archie. You were well taught," Phil praised the pig and lifted him into the lorry. Reunited the pig and the man drove off, heading for Liverpool and the ferry home to Ireland.

As the night fell Charles Emdyke felt very satisfied with his day's work. He had been in contact with a local pork production facility and made a deal that would give him a threefold return on his investment. In joyful mood he carried out a large, circular tin of kitchen scraps to feed "Archie", whom he thought was still in the rear garden. The pig had, of course, escaped leaving only the remains of the rope halter as evidence of what had happened. At first the idea of the pig escaping didn't concern Emdyke greatly because the fields and farmyard provided plenty of hiding places. He was certain that "Archie" had not gone very far away and that he would show himself again when he was hungry.

With two of his stock workers Charles decided that he would go to the large sty and observe his other purchases. He was both shocked and surprised to find that the large door to the sty had been broken off its hinges and was lying on the ground. The gate that led into pig enclosures was still intact, but instead of hearing the grunting of a herd of pigs, there was silence. He ran into the enclosures and through the sty only to find that it was empty. All the feed that had been put into the troughs the previous evening had gone and the troughs themselves had been licked clean. Emdyke was at a loss to explain what his eyes were witnessing. All the Irish pigs he had bought off Phil and he had absolutely no idea where they had gone.

There were loud voices shouting from the other side of the farm buildings and Charles hurried to see what had caused such an alarm. "Boss! Boss! Quick!" came the cries and Emdyke became increasingly concerned that something had happened.

"What has happened?" he called out.

"Over there," one of the men cried out and pointed up to the hills behind the farmhouse. Charles could see that there was a terrible commotion on the hill, with people running wildly, shouting at the top of their voices. At first it wasn't clear what was happening and Charles led his workers toward the crowd. This was the Yorkshire countryside and totally unused to such commotion. But he did wonder if it had anything to do with his pigs, though he soon put such concerns to the back of his mind. After all, for his pigs to escape the enclosure they would have had to clear a wall that was over four feet in height. It was hardly credible that any pig could achieve such a leap.

As he came closer to one of his neighbours Charles asked, "What's happening?" By this time he was panting for breath and exhausted by the effort he had made to reach the crowd.

"Pigs? Wild Monsters!" the neighbour shouted. "They have rooted up and destroyed every bean, turnip, and vegetable field for miles."

"Oh my God!" exclaimed Emdyke as he slowly regained his breath.

"We just might need God's help against these Devil Pigs," he was told. "Every kitchen garden, cornfield and lawn has been torn up by these creatures, wherever they came from"

All around him Charles could here the yelps and barking of dogs as they chased their quarry. These pigs, however, were very quick, very tough and very vicious. As the men and dogs chased them, they would occasionally turn on their pursuers, injuring them severely. When Charles caught his first sight of the "Demon Pigs" he realised